THE
RELUCTANT
TIME
TRAVELLER

JANIS MACKAY

Kelpies

To Ian
with love and gratitude

Kelpies is an imprint of Floris Books
First published in 2014 by Floris Books
© 2014 Janis Mackay

Janis Mackay has asserted her right under the
Copyright, Designs and Patent Act 1988 to
be identified as the Author of this work.

This publisher acknowledges subsidy from
Creative Scotland towards the publication of this volume

 This book is also available
as an eBook

British Library CIP data available
ISBN 978-178250-111-4
Printed in Poland

PROLOGUE

'Help!' I try to shout, but 'Help!' is stuck in my mouth! A loud buzzing is ringing in my head. I can't see a thing. I shut my eyes, open my eyes; both ways it's black. The buzzing keeps on. Maybe I've landed in a wasp's nest? My head feels like it's going to burst. I stick my hands out and hit something hard. What? Where am I? I fumble behind, to the side. I'm hemmed in, trapped in a tiny space – a box, or a cupboard. I try again to shout for help but my voice won't work, like it hasn't caught up with me. I push my elbows out, trying to break open this box. Ow! My funny bones throb. Maybe I'm in a coffin? Maybe the time travel hasn't worked and I'm buried alive? I always knew this was a bad idea.

"Help!" A tiny squeal comes out. That's my voice. It's catching up with me.

Ok. I'm standing, so I can't be in a coffin, which is a relief. But where am I? I listen for clues but all I can hear is my heart drumming like mad and more squeaks coming out of my mouth. I thrash out and grab hold of what feels like a pole. I pat it all the way down. At the bottom it feels scratchy, like a broom. Even though I am in the worst ever nightmare, I laugh. I, Saul Martin, not exactly famous for cleaning the house, am trapped in some box with a beloved broom. The laugh comes out squeaky. But when you're in a tight corner any kind of laugh works wonders. I stop panicking and force myself to get a grip and think.

I don't feel dead. Maybe this is some kind of cleaning cupboard? I take a deep breath. Bad idea: a bleachy smell clings to my throat. With one hand clamped over my mouth, I reach out again. Behind me is what feels like a mop. Next to my feet is what I think is a tin bucket. But where is Agnes Brown, my companion in time travel? Because one thing is pretty clear – she's not in the cupboard. Off to explore history by herself, probably, with her kit bag and her total dedication. Agnes has gone and left me behind. We'd had our hands pressed against the bark of the yew tree, preparing to zoom back through time, and I'd said to her, "You've got to really want it, remember." But really I'd been talking to myself. Agnes had no doubts. She did want it. Thousand per cent. She really, really wanted to travel back in time. She wasn't scared.

I was. I mean, have you ever stopped to think what you'd do if you were time travelling and something went wrong? You can't exactly phone your mum and say, "Hey Mum, can you pick me up from 1914? Pleeeeeease?" I gulp, hoping this *is* 1914. I don't know where I am. I don't know when. I don't know anything. Agnes and I are separated and I am in serious time-travel trouble.

I bang my fist on the door of the cleaning-cupboard-box. "Help!" I shout, and this time it sounds like me – freaked, but at least not squeaking. My voice has caught up. "HELP ME!" I roar and bang again, not caring who might discover me. I have to get out.

I can hear footsteps. Little feet, short steps. They're coming closer. Then they stop.

"Whit the heck's that, eh?" It's a girl, but not Agnes. Her voice sounds as snappy as her footsteps.

"Hello!" I call out desperately, my face pressing up against the wooden door. It smells like tar. "Could you let me out?" Whoever is out there takes a step closer. Phew.

"Somebody playing a trick on me, eh? We all get a laugh out of scaring poor wee Elsie to death, eh? Well, let me tell you for nothing, Elsie here is sick of it."

"No!" I yell, banging on the wood. "It's not a trick. Please, let me out of here."

"Are you a ghostie? Eh?"

"No, I'm a… a boy." I try to sound friendly but my voice comes out whiny. I probably sound like a ghost. "Please, Elsie," I plead, "just let me out."

"Whit kind of boy? One whit's up to no good, I'll bet. A boy whit's a scoundrel, a thief, a rascal, eh? Bet you pinched a sugar lump from the maister's sugar bowl. He'd whip you and lock you up for that."

"No, honest," I whine, "I didn't pinch anything. I'm just a normal boy. My name's Saul."

I can hear her rattle something. Keys, I hope. "Come on, hurry up," I cry out, banging frantically. "Open the door. It stinks in here."

"Huld yer horses," she snaps. "Gaunt doesn't like varmints. Not one bit." She's whispering now. I pictured a little old-fashioned face pressed up close to the other side of the door. "Yer lucky he didn't shove you in the cupboard that's got the hares dripping blood. Yea think the mop cupboard reeks? Ha! Wait till he locks you in the hanging cupboard." I can hear the key half turn then stop. "Yer probably one of they spies. It's all they talk about in town. War this, war that. It's coming, that's whit they're saying. Spies creeping everywhere. Yer one of the enemies, I bet."

"Listen," I hiss, not knowing what she means by 'Gaunt' or 'varmints', but knowing a bit about spies and enemies. I try to sound chilled. "Elsie, it's ok, I'm not going to hurt you. Nobody locked me up. This looks worse than it is. I just… got lost. It happens, and I'm not a spy. I'm… from here. Let me out. I'm not the enemy, honest."

"So you never did nothing bad?"

"No!" I wail, except right now I am feeling guilty. I feel everything would have been ok if I'd been more up for this time travel, all bold and certain like Agnes. At least then I wouldn't have to deal with this on my own. I pressed my cheek against the smelly wood and groaned. I had never really wanted this. I wanted to stay at home. We are going on the school trip to Paris in two weeks and I am seriously looking forward to that. That's travel. Hurtling back in time is not what you see in travel programmes, not what you see pictures of in a travel agent's, and not the travel I need. I didn't think that to learn about the First World War, we actually had to pay it a visit. Though Agnes thinks it's a great idea. And she also wants to find out who really owns the land our den is on now. Our den is about to be bulldozed, and she is dead keen on saving it. Which I get. I want to save it too. But still, I should have put my foot down. I should have said: 'Time travel is a totally dangerous, mad idea. N. O. NO!'

"No," I whimper again, "let me out, Elsie, please." Why had I not said no to Agnes? If I had, I'd be lounging on my beanbag in my room, sending messages to Will and Robbie like usual, or playing my Xbox, not locked in some old smelly cupboard wondering if I'll ever get out. I'd said "Yes, alright then" to time travel – but I'd said it reluctantly. That's what Agnes calls my swithering and doubts: *reluctance*. Whatever you call it, she had none of it. And, like I said, she vanished off to 1914 and I was left standing alone at the yew tree. Where is she now? And where am I? This Elsie person speaks funny. *Is* it 1914? I can hardly ask.

"Please, Elsie," I beg, "just open the door. I'm all confused. It's pitch dark in here. I don't know if it's day or night." This silly titter bursts out of me. "I don't even know what year it is."

"You're daft as a brush. I'm not telling the enemy nothing. We've been told: keep mum."

"I'm not the enemy, ok?"

"Whit? You talk like the enemy."

It's hard to keep my voice calm when I feel like kicking the door down and yelling at her. "I'm just a normal boy," I plead.

"Normal boys don't go getting themselves locked in the broom cupboard. It's not worth my bacon to let you out. Whit did you do if you didn't pinch something, eh?" She stops ranting to having a little coughing fit.

When the coughing stops, the ranting starts again. "Begging at the gates, eh? Gaunt can't abide they dirty beggars. Not one bit."

And I can't abide this one bit. I kick the door and hear something clatter. My foot throbs.

"Whit you doing with my mop bucket, eh?" She sounds angry now. "You kick a dent in that bucket and it'll be me, poor Elsie Noble, whit will forfeit her shilling. Now stop it, you hear?" Which gives me an idea. I lash out again and the tin bucket clangs. "You dirty little sneak," she yells, pulling back the door. Result! I blink at the sudden light. "You leave my good bucket alone!"

I see this small face peer in, topped by a frilly white cap. She's only about ten. She looks like a maid – a very wee pale one. I jump over the bucket, dart round her and speed down a corridor.

"Halt, you!" she shouts.

I pelt along the corridor, taking bleach-free breaths, but can't hear her chasing me. There are loads of doors. Where am I? Maybe I have got something right and this is the big house. The big house that's a ruin in 2014, with a big old garden no one's using, and where we have our den. Maybe I really have managed to travel back one hundred years and Agnes Brown is somewhere close. I seriously hope so.

Behind me I can hear little Elsie fumbling with her bucket and calling out: "I'm off to report you to Mrs Buchan! Lucky for you Gaunt's awa' from home. But the housekeeper will send you packing, so she will, and give you a thick ear while she's at it. I might be half-pint size, but not Mrs Buchan. You scared the living daylights out o' me. I thought you wis the Hun."

What does she mean, 'the Hun'? Am I a Hun? Who's Gaunt? Who's Mrs Buchan? And *where* is my time-travelling buddy, Agnes Brown?

1

The sun streamed through the classroom window. It was so bright I couldn't even see the Smart board. The teacher was talking about wind energy, I think: giant turbines, people protesting about having them on the hills here in the Borders, that kind of thing. But all I could think about was the school trip to France. It was going to be great.

Except, before the French trip, I went somewhere else. Actually, I went some*time* else.

To explain how I ended up running away from a wee maid called Elsie, I need to go back a few days... or, maybe that should be forward a hundred years? When you're a time traveller, talking about time gets a bit confusing. Let's just say, in June 2014, I wasn't concentrating on wind energy. Instead I was gazing up at this fly on the classroom ceiling thinking about being up the Eiffel Tower with all my pals. Next thing a paper plane flew in an impressive arc from the back of the room and landed right on my lap. Just in time, because the teacher turned round from the Smart board, sniffing, like she smelt nonsense going on.

A message. When the teacher turned back, I unfolded the wings of the plane without rustling it, and opened out the sleek paper body. There were just two words followed by a huge curly question mark:

Time Travel **?**

I scrunched up the paper plane. I'd always known she would suggest this, sooner or later. I would have been fine just living in the ordinary present. I mean, that was enough, what with the twins – loudest one-year-olds ever – and high school (our first year was just finishing) and the gang and the summer holidays coming up. But having Agnes Brown in my gang was never going to be ordinary. Or easy.

"Just once, Saul," she said, tipping her head sideways so her long dark hair swung down.

"Nah, I don't know," I said. We were in the overgrown garden in front of our gang hut, just me and her, after school. We were trying to remember how the time traveller, our friend Agatha Black, had made fire, but rubbing stones together wasn't working. Agnes had a packet of marshmallows with her for toasting. Good thing I had matches.

"But you know the time travel formula. Come on Saul, you can't just pass up the opportunity of the century."

She straightened her head and gave me the 'I dare you' look. I'd climbed right to the top of the oak tree because of that look. I'd skipped school because of that look. I'd swum in the freezing River Tweed in March because of that look. I pulled the scrunched-up paper plane from my pocket, hunched down and stuffed it under our spire of twigs. Then I struck a match and lit the plane. Orange flames shot up, licked onto the twigs, and soon the fire was roaring. The stones we'd been madly rubbing together lay at the side of our bonfire, all scratched and useless.

"It's dangerous and you don't know what you're asking." I tossed a twig onto the fire.

"Don't you think Agatha would want us to carry on the tradition?"

"What tradition?"

Agnes was stabbing a marshmallow onto the end of a sharp twig. "The time-traveller tradition, of course."

"Oh, that." I laughed, like it was no big deal. "I thought you meant the ride-a-bike-off-a-cliff tradition."

"Yeah, now *that* would be dangerous." Nibbling a pink gooey marshmallow, she pulled her diary from the back pocket of her jeans. She propped her toasting twig on one of the stones and flicked through the pages. Agnes was always writing in that diary, or reading it, or drawing little diagrams. "Time-traveller formula," she announced, then flashed me her 'Are you paying attention?' look. She read:

Earth
Fire
Swirling water
Rainbow vapours
Yew tree
Gold and, last but not least,
An antique song.

When elements are vibrating in harmony, in tune with planets, it is possible to slip through the doors of time.

She winked at me. "It'll be an adventure!"

"Might be, might not be, and anyway, you forgot the most important bit of the formula." I got busy with my marshmallow and squatted down beside her, and she moved her diary away, like I might spy or something. "But I'm not going to tell you what it is. I can have secrets too."

Agnes shrugged. "I write seriously bad poetry, Saul," she said, turning pink. "That's all."

I believed her. Agnes was the type to write poetry, probably seriously good. We sat not speaking for a while, toasting marshmallows, watching the flames, feeling the sun and the fire warm on our faces, and I bet we were both thinking about Agatha Black. I know I was. We both agreed she was the most adventurous person we had ever met. Agatha Black had travelled two centuries, just to see what the future was like! She had slept in our gang hut on her own. That was the winter before last when the whole overgrown garden had been covered in snow. Now it was summer. It was warm. The garden was a green wild mess with weeds galore. It was light until late at night, but there's still no way you'd get me spending the night in our gang hut. Agatha was brave.

"Don't you want to see what it's like, Saul?"

I stared into the flames. I did want to see the past, and I knew how to do it. But so much could go wrong. Not that Agnes thought about that. Agnes Brown wasn't scared of anything. She'd had a lifetime of being different. I mean, she lived in a caravan at the back of the garage and her dad was this bearded grungy guy who played the fiddle on the street corner to make money. Compared with Agnes, I was pretty normal.

"I've got gold," Agnes said, holding up her hand and turning her fingers round. Her ring flashed in the sunlight. She inherited it from her grandma and her mother. "Tell me what the other thing is? The thing from the time-travel formula that I forgot. Come on," she nudged me. "Saul?"

I made her wait till I'd scoffed my marshmallow.

"It is: you have to really, really, really want it," I told her, eventually, "and you have to totally believe it will happen. Faith," I said, feeling my heart skip a beat, "is the most important thing." The fire crackled. I did want to time travel. I just didn't know if I *really* wanted to. Like really, really! I did believe it could happen, but so much could go wrong. I guess I didn't have faith. A gust of wind blew suddenly, which was weird because it was a still day.

"Well, I have faith," Agnes boasted. "Do you?"

I didn't answer.

"Oh, come on, Saul. Let's!"

"I don't think Agatha would appreciate us just dropping in. She said it herself, didn't she? She kept saying she had her life to live. Well, we've got ours." I said all this to the fire. I didn't exactly feel great being scared, especially seeing as I was the gang leader. But I was. Scared, that is. The thought of hurtling back through time was freaking me out.

"I'm not thinking of us going back to see Agatha." And then she came out with it; the real reason for all this.

"It's the den and this old ruined house, and the garden. We could save it. My gran says if the title deeds of this house could be found, the property developers could be stopped. Saul—" Agnes was practically shouting by now; her eyes were shiny and her face was red. "This is our childhood we're talking about. The gang. The trees. Freedom. Everything. My gran said she wouldn't be surprised if bulldozers came in any day. No one has claimed this land for one hundred years, so the council are selling it. And my gran, she says..." Agnes lowered her voice (her gran is famous for saying pretty weird things) "...she says, by rights, this land should belong to *my family*. She says it was wrongfully taken out of our hands, that it was lost after my great-great-great grandfather died in about 1914." She stared at me across the flames. "Might be total rubbish. Probably is, but we have to do something. We can't just lie back and watch our den being pulped and the garden being dug up and fancy big houses being built for rich folks. It's not fair. Come on, Saul. We could travel back to 1914. See what we can find." Like I said, Agnes isn't scared of anything. I looked at her through the crackling fire and she smiled at me, like this was some little day trip to North Berwick she was suggesting.

I felt sorry for Agnes's gran. If I lived in a caravan I would make up stories too. I'd be telling the world how my other house was a castle. "What's 'title deeds' anyway?" I mumbled, poking the fire with a stick.

"Something like a scroll of paper," she said, all excited. "It says on it who owns the house, and land and this den. You know, official documents. And if we want to save this den, we need to find them. Somebody has to own this place."

"Dunno," I muttered. 1914! Jeez! We could land in the muddy trenches of the First World War, then get gassed. We could materialise right in front of a charging horse. We could get a bayonet stuck in our hands and be ordered to fight on the front line. Or we could get the time thing all wrong and end up in ancient history. We could get taken away by the body snatchers. Or get locked in the stocks with rotten eggs flung in our faces. We could catch the plague. We might hurtle back centuries and end up in some gladiator ring. Or get trampled by a dinosaur. Even worse, we could get stuck in in-between time and never get back.

A pine cone flew above my head and landed in the fire, which snapped me out of my morbid thoughts. I could hear Agnes behind me.

"Oh well," she said, breezily, "if you're so reluctant, Saul, maybe I'll go by myself. I've got the formula too, don't forget. And I am related to Agatha's dad, the great time traveller Albert Black."

I swung round just in time to see her disappear through the hole in the hedge. "He wasn't great," I shouted after her. "Actually he got quite a lot of things wrong."

"Well, maybe he did. It doesn't mean we will. And I care about this place," she shouted from behind the old garden wall. "I want to save the den!"

"So do I!" I yelled to the wall.

"Well, let's do it then," she yelled back. "Let's go to 1914!"

2

"Who can tell me this? Hmm?" The history teacher threw me a long look, meaning 'Saul Martin surely can.' This has happened ever since I won the history essay competition last year. I wriggled in my seat.

"Yeah," Robbie whispered next to me. "Go on mastermind. Dazzle her with your brilliance!"

The teacher fired her question, "When did the the First World War begin?"

I relaxed. That wasn't a difficult question. Even Robbie knew that. He stuck his hand up, panting the way he did when he was desperate to give an answer. But the teacher wasn't looking at him. "Saul? Will you kindly tell us?"

"1914," I answered.

Robbie couldn't contain himself. "That was a hundred years ago, Mrs Johnston."

"Exactly," she said. "And when did it end?"

I knew that too. Robbie obviously didn't because he lowered his hand and stopped panting like a dog. But Mrs Johnston wasn't looking at Robbie or me. She was staring at Agnes. Agnes was the genius of the class who sat at the back and rarely said a word. But since she joined our gang she'd stopped being invisible, or bullied. People looked at her now as if she was special, instead of weird.

"The Armistice was signed on November the 11th, 1918," answered Agnes, quietly, then added into the impressed silence, "at 11 a.m."

"Exactly, Agnes," said Mrs Johnston. "And this year is the centenary of the beginning of the First World War, as Robbie said." Robbie beamed round at the class, well pleased. The teacher though, looked a bit sad. "It is a fitting time to remember the soldiers, service men and women who died or were wounded." Mrs Johnston had our attention. It was something about the quietness of her voice, and the sad look in her eyes. "Many soldiers in the First World War were very young," she went on. "Many still teenagers – the same age as some of your big brothers – when they left their homes and families. Many were killed. Even more suffered injuries that changed their lives. Families lost sons, brothers, fathers, uncles. In Peebleshire alone, over five hundred men were killed in the First World War. That's like the whole school. Can you imagine? It was a terrible loss of innocence and of lives. Remembrance is about understanding how we cope with sadness and loss."

I could hear Robbie rummaging in his bag. He's famous for his extravagant snacks. I spied a huge packet of crisps. "And why would young men and boys march off to war?" The teacher was looking at me again, but I was thinking about cheese and onion crisps.

"Dunno," I mumbled. I had no idea why teenagers would want to sleep in muddy trenches among the rats, knowing that at any moment they might get shot. The teacher scanned the room but nobody answered.

"Um, to do their *duty*, maybe?" Nathan said, uncertainly.

"Yes, that's one of the reasons." Mrs Johnston showed us this huge poster with a fierce-looking man pointing his finger. Written underneath was:

YOUR COUNTRY NEEDS

YOU!

"Well, I wouldn't go," said Will, "it's madness." And that started a bit of an argument with some people in the class saying they would go and most saying they wouldn't, and ended with the teacher saying it was a very different world one hundred years ago.

"It is important we remember this war. It is sometimes called 'the Great War'. 'Great' here means big, it means terrible. Young men were so enthusiastic to be a part of it. Not that they understood what it meant at the time. At the beginning, people were saying it would be over by Christmas, but it wasn't. It went on for four years. Can you imagine? So many young men dying. Others coming back blind and lame.

"Listen", the teacher went on, opening a book. "This is the beginning of a famous poem. It was written by Wilfred Owen, a poet and a soldier of the First World War.

Bent double, like old beggars under sacks,
Knock-kneed, coughing like hags, we cursed through sludge,
Till on the haunting flares we turned our backs,
And towards our distant rest began to trudge.

Men marched asleep. Many had lost their boots,
But limped on, blood-shod. All went lame; all blind;
Drunk with fatigue; deaf even to the hoots
Of gas-shells dropping softly behind."

No one said anything. I think Mrs Johnston was going to go on, but the bell rang for break time. Relieved, we dashed outside into the playground. Robbie wanted to play war games. He wanted us to clamber up the rope assault course. "Bang!" he shouted, pointing two fingers at me. I crumpled to my knees, groaning and clasping my chest.

Next thing Agnes was on her knees next to me, like she was some kind of army nurse. "Changed your mind, Saul?" she whispered then bit into an apple. I swallowed hard, lying there on the grass next to the climbing frame, but she didn't wait for an answer. "If we go back to 1914 to find the title deeds for the old house, we'll also get to understand more about the war. We could find out why all those people went. Why they were willing to *die*. Don't you want to know?"

I shrugged. To be really honest, I didn't.

"Hey, don't look so worried," Agnes poked me. "This is Scotland, remember. All the fighting happened far away. I've read about it in novels. The muddy trenches of the Western Front, the fields of Flanders. That's like in France and Belgium and those kind of places. We'll be fine!" She took another bite of her rosy apple then with bulging cheeks said, "Go on, Saul; let's time travel."

"Ok," I said, reluctantly. Then Robbie ran up and shot me.

3

When I got home that day I stared for ages at the photo of me and Mum and Dad in the hallway. That photo had been taken before the twins came along. I was about nine, and grinning, and Mum and Dad had their faces pressed up against mine. I felt a lump in my throat. What if something went wrong and I never saw them again?

"You ok, Saul?" Mum said at teatime. I had begged for my favourite scampi and chips, thinking there might not be many teatimes left, but now it was in front of me I couldn't eat it. Normally I love scampi and chips. I remembered Agatha telling me about her favourite food when she was visiting from 1812. My stomach heaved. Pigeons! There is no way I would eat a pigeon.

"Feel a bit funny," I whined.

"Tell us a joke then, Saul," said Dad, biting into a chip and winking at me.

Ellie and Esme had already been fed and were romping around in their playpen. I tried to think of a joke but could only come up with baby ones. "Knock-knock," I said.

"Who's there?" Mum and Dad both chanted.

"Doctor," I said.

Dad speared another chip and whizzed it through the air. "Doctor Who!" he said, laughing.

"Who's been in that Tardis zooming through time for over fifty years," Mum said. "Poor guy doesn't know if he's going or coming." I gulped. "Eat a chip, Saul. You're probably just feeling nervous about going to France."

"It'll be fantastique!" Dad said, in a funny accent. "You'll come back asking for frog's legs. That's what they eat in France, did you know that, son?"

I shook my head and gulped again. Suddenly pigeons didn't sound so bad. I picked up my fork, tried to forget about zooming through time, and stabbed a chip.

I was allowed to go out after tea. If I was going to get lost in time I wanted to spend as much time in the den as possible. It was the best place ever. I met Will and Robbie at the corner of the street and we headed off. We had about five different ways of getting there, to put people off the trail, just in case they got suspicious and followed us.

"Can't wait till we actually get to France," Will said. We were jumping off walls and doing jumps up and down steps.

"Too right. Bon jour monsieur," Robbie said, then he tried to jump over somebody's front doorstep and tripped. "Ow!" he yelled.

Ten minutes later we reached the crumbling hole in the wall. We did our usual check over our shoulders. No one was following us. Being the gang leader I went first. Once I was through the hole in the wall I wriggled through a gap in the thick jagged hedge that ran around the abandoned garden. The others wriggled through after me. We slumped on the long clumpy grass. It always felt magical, arriving in our secret garden. It was a pretty big garden and down the end there were a few walls still standing from a falling-down house. That was fenced off with

and

signs all over it. It would have been a big posh place once. We all loved our den, even though there was this black cloud hanging over it. It wasn't only Agnes's gran talking doom and gloom. Robbie said any day now there would be 'For Sale' signs, then bulldozers rolling in. Our den would be flattened along with those last walls of the ruined house; luxury villas would take over all this space, even the yew tree would go.

But Robbie gets a lot of stuff wrong. So does Agnes's gran. More worrying was Will saying *his* granny said the same thing. That's seriously bad news: Will's granny is like our prophet. She gets a lot of things right.

But right now I wasn't wanting to think about luxury villas, chain-sawed trees and the end of the den. I was the gang leader and we were the coolest gang in Peebles. We had our hut where we hung out, then there was the garden, though maybe 'wilderness' is a better word for it. Or Scottish jungle. It's mostly jagged briars but you can see it was once a proper garden. There's a huge yew tree in the middle – the one we used when we were getting Agatha back to 1812. I think it helped with time travel because it's really old. I don't know how old, but a lot older than 1812, because when Agatha was in her own time she carved her initials in it: $\mathcal{AB}$. Whenever I start thinking that Agatha Black coming here was just a dream, I look at that tree. Yew trees live for hundreds of years, heaps longer than people. There's one in Perthshire that's two thousand years old! True. It even says so in Wikipedia.

Will says his granny told him nobody knows who owns this garden and the house. That's why it's gone to wrack and ruin. That's why the council plan to sell it off. Me and Will and Robbie never go near the creepy old house. It's just some crumbling rooms, surrounded by barbed wire. Crows and mice live in it. Our den is the old wooden shed on the edge of the garden. Robbie gave it the name Pisa because it leans to the side, like a tower in Italy, he said.

"Where's Agnes?" Will asked, once we got our breath back.

"Probably already in the den scribbling in that secret diary of hers," Robbie said. "She always gets here early."

He jumped to his feet and ran to the den. "Agnes!" he yelled.

Two seconds later he backed out of the den, looking a bit shaken. "She's not here, but… there's this stuff."

I got this fluttery feeling in my tummy, imagining what kind of stuff. Will ran but I hung back, racking my brains for what to tell them. We were a gang. We had all kinds of truth pacts. "What's this about then, Saul?" Robbie pointed to the corner of the shed. Agnes had been busy. A bowl of earth. A bowl of water. A glass globe. A candle.

I gulped.

Will and Robbie, standing over all the time-travel implements, turned to face me. I was in the doorway, struggling. "So, Saul." Will said, slowly, "you planning on going somewhere?"

"Without telling us?" Robbie added. They both folded their arms and waited for me to speak.

4

I just stood there, at the door of our den, wondering what to tell them.

"I knew you would go one of these days," Will said. "I mean, you've got the formula. It would be mad not to go. I'm surprised you waited this long."

"Rather you than me," Robbie said.

I felt this huge relief. They were ok about it. They weren't mad at me. I grinned.

"I was going to tell you," I said, striding into the shed and sitting down. We had done the place up when we first found it and made it our den: crates for chairs and a box for a table. We even had a few old cushions scattered about. Robbie and Will plonked themselves down too.

"Yeah, send us a postcard from history, won't you?" Robbie said, then he was reaching over and slapping me on the back, like I was the brave hero. "Jeez," he said, "Are you not totally terrified? I mean, sometimes I can't sleep for thinking about those body snatchers."

Yes, actually I was totally terrified. I blurted out, "It was Agnes's idea. She was the one who said we should go. She's got this idea that we should go back one hundred years. She said it would be the adventure of the century. And not just that – we could save the den. She said, if we could find the deeds of this place – like find out who really owns the old garden – we could stop them building on this land. She said –"

"*She's* going with you?" they chorused.

"Um… yeah." Then, because we were a gang, and because it was one of our rules, I said, "Do you want to come too?"

All for one, and all that.

They looked at me.

They looked at each other.

Then they looked at the ground, and muttered, "Thanks, but no thanks." That was Robbie.

"Nah, thanks for asking, but yeah, I mean, no. Yeah, no thanks." That was Will. "We'll look after things here."

Robbie nodded like that was a genius idea. They were both gazing at me.

"So, when you going?" Robbie asked.

Just then we heard three short whistles from the other side of the hedge – our gang signal. We bustled out of the den to see Agnes, with leaves in her hair, wriggling through the hole in the hedge. She had a tin whistle in her hand. The antique song, I thought.

"Saul has been telling us about the big time travel plan," Robbie didn't hang about.

"Yeah," said Will, "so, when you going?"

Agnes looked at me, and shrugged. "Ask Saul," she said. "He's the gang leader."

I shaded my eyes with my hand and studied the sun,

as though I was some ancient astronomer reading the heavens. I pulled at my chin and tried to look casual, but inside my brain was racing. "Well…" I blinked. "Um, soon," I announced.

"Tomorrow," said Agnes, and she smiled at me. My tummy turned over. Then she nipped into the den and appeared two seconds later without her tin whistle. I pictured it lying next to the bowl of water, ready to hurtle us back in time. "So," she clapped her hands, "while we're still here, fancy a game of hide and seek?"

I leant against the den and counted to one hundred. I found Robbie and Will right away, in their usual hiding places behind trees with their elbows sticking out. Then the three of us went looking for Agnes. We tried all the usual spots: behind the den, behind the bushes, under the hedge, behind the trees. We even looked up the trees.

"Bet she's in the creepy old house," Will said, lowering his voice and pointing to the ruin.

Robbie whipped out his phone to see whether his mum had conveniently texted him to come home. As far as I could see, the screen was blank. "I need to go soon," he told us. We all stared at the dark ruin. "She knows it's out of bounds," Robbie hissed. "It's condemned."

"That wouldn't stop her," Will whispered.

I didn't want it to stop me either. "As gang leader," I declared, "I say we look for ten more minutes, ok? We'll enter the ruin together and check the rooms, or – what's left of them, ha-ha!" They didn't seem to find that funny. "If we don't find her after ten minutes we'll shout for her to come out." I shot Robbie a look. "Then you can go home."

"Ok," Will agreed.

Robbie didn't look too happy but he grunted, nodded, and off we went.

"We're coming to get you, Agnes," Will sang.

"Quit the scary stuff," Robbie elbowed him. Shoulder to shoulder we stepped over the barbed wire. I tried not looking at the sign:

**DANGER
KEEP OUT**

To get into the ruin we clambered through a window that had no glass. A bird inside screeched and flew over our heads out the window. Will yelled and grabbed me.

"It's only a pigeon," said Robbie, panting. "Calm down."

The three of us stood in the ancient hallway, getting used to the dim light, and taking in the place. No way would I have come into this ruin before. But actually it was starting to feel pretty adventurous. Cobwebs hung from what was left of the ceiling. Bits of the garden had come into the house. Weeds pushed up through the floor tiles. You could see patches of blue sky alongside the broken oak beams above. Heavy wooden doors hung from hinges. Bits of wallpaper curled down from caved-in walls. We inched forward and peered into a room, lined with shelves, all falling down, the books on them rotting. "Maybe this was a study," I whispered. A big leather armchair looked like it was now the home to dozens of mice. An old-fashioned gaslight fitting teetered above the massive marble mantelpiece.

The room was full of bird poo. It stank. We side-stepped around the edge of the floor, I pushed another door and we found ourselves in what must have been a bedroom. You could see the fireplace and the remains of an old iron bed. We kept nervously glancing up, like the ceiling could cave in any minute.

"Agnes isn't in here," I whispered.

But then it was like we forgot we were in a creepy old ruin and started having fun. If the ceilings hadn't completely caved in yet it would be a sad coincidence if they did now. Will ran around squawking like a mad bird and me and Robbie pretended to ponder the rotting book titles. In the hall there was the bottom of a huge sweeping staircase but half the stairs were broken and the banister had fallen over. After mucking about, I felt more confident; I pushed open a couple more creaking doors. There were cupboards with broken plates on the floor. Another cupboard had a broom and an old tin bucket in it.

Robbie pushed open a door that said

"Somebody's initials," he whispered. "Will Calder, for instance…" Will giggled, "…or Winston Churchill."

"It's not anybody's initials, stupid," I said, "it means

'toilet.'" Robbie kicked the door and we snuck in. A cast iron bath lay on its side. There was a cracked old toilet in the corner. What a dump.

"Right. That's ten minutes," Robbie whispered, urgently. "She's not here. Let's go."

He was backing out and dragging me with him when I heard a giggle. The bath moved slightly. Will gasped. Robbie grabbed me, and Agnes Brown clambered out of the old bath, brushing herself down. Dust puffed off her clothes.

"I thought you'd never find me," she said, then looked up and grinned at us. "What took you so long?"

Then a mouse or rat squeaked right there in the room. We all yelled and bolted out past the study, along the hallway and practically leapt out the window. We scrambled over the barbed wire and didn't stop running until we reached the den. "That – was – gross," Robbie panted.

"Totally vile," said Will.

"Are you so desperate to have a bath, Agnes?" I said, though right away I felt bad, because Agnes didn't have a bath, or a shower. She lived with her dad and granny in a caravan behind the petrol station. She'd told me that to have a bath they all trouped off to a friend of her gran's twice a week with a bar of soap and towels.

But Agnes just laughed and that set us all off, out of relief probably, after being in the creepy old ruin.

"What's that?" Agnes stopped laughing. We all froze. It sounded like someone was pushing their way through the hole in the hedge. "Somebody's coming," she whispered.

5

It was like we were turned to stone. The four of us just stared at the hedge. Someone or something was pushing through the hole at the bottom of it. Next thing a man in a high vis yellow jacket appeared, puffing and patting himself down.

"You shouldn't be playing around here," he said, looking taken aback at seeing us. He stood up tall and waved us away like we were annoying insects. "This is a demolition site. Off you go."

I stepped forward. Actually Robbie pushed me forward. "No, it's not. This is our gang hut," I said. My heart was racing. "We don't go near the demolition site." That was a whopper. We had just come from there. I nodded to the shed. "That's our den. We've had it for three years."

"It's the best," Will added.

"Totally," chipped in Robbie. "It's called 'Pisa.'"

The man looked at him like he was crazy.

"Please don't take it away from us," Agnes said.

The man was already fishing gadgets out of his pocket. "We've to measure up this dump. So kiddies, it's time to say bye-bye to your playpen. Work starts here in a week. We'll get this mess sorted."

"It's not a playpen, it's a den. And you don't know who owns this land," Agnes piped up.

"Well little madam, I know one thing," the man said, "you don't! Now scoot!"

Then he marched past us. I couldn't believe he was striding into our garden like it was just anywhere.

"But – you can't!" Agnes shouted after him.

The man stopped and looked back at us over his shoulder. "I'm not saying I don't feel sorry for you, kiddies, but the law is the law." He strode on through the garden. Agnes pulled my sleeve.

"We really have to go back in time now, Saul. Even if we're scared. Even if it's dangerous. We have to."

"She's right," Robbie said, "you're the gang leader, Saul. You can't let them just march in here and wreck everything."

I didn't like leaving the den with a stranger snooping around. The four of us walked back across the field, down the lane and into the town. We were all silent and you could feel this sadness sitting over us. It was Will who broke the silence. "A week is a week." He was trying to sound upbeat. "I mean, maybe we've got time to save the den."

"Yeah, all the time in history," I said, sarcastically. "And what if we disappear to 1914 for more than a week? We might be too late: even if we can find out who owns this land – which is unlikely – what difference will it make? It will all be bulldozed when we get back."

"I think what happens," Will said, still trying to sound all positive, "is that you go into a time warp.

So even if days go by in the other time, only seconds have passed in your normal time." Will was the most scientific in the gang. He thought about these things. And when he came up with these wee lectures, we usually listened.

"That would come in handy," I said. "To be away for a week and back in a minute. Best of both worlds: go and not go! Or is that best of both times?"

We were coming to the corner in town where we usually split and go our separate ways home. We slowed down and waited for Will to come up with more lecture. He did. "It's like, you've got this ancient formula that cracks open time and lets you slip through. The time you go back to has already been, so you can visit it. But the future hasn't. You don't lose time. Get it?" Robbie looked perplexed. Agnes looked curious. I was beginning to look hopeful. "It's like," Will went on, looking excited now, "you could be gone into history for ages, except it won't be ages. It'll feel like it, but it won't be any time at all! You'll be there and back in no time," he grinned. "We won't even miss you!"

The next morning I gave Mum a hug and she looked at me strangely because I don't usually go round giving her hugs. Then she laughed and kissed me on the nose. I stood waving to Dad for ages when he went off in his taxi. Then I wanted to help feed the twins, but Mum said why didn't I run off and enjoy myself. "Have a good time," that's what she actually said, "it's the longest day of the year – make the most of it!"

So Agnes and I were by the yew tree. The man with

the high-vis yellow jacket was, thankfully, nowhere to be seen. There was a bulldozer parked up by the wall, waiting to charge in and flatten everything, but Will said by law they had to wait six days. I'm not sure how Will could know that. I wasn't sure about anything.

Agnes though looked sure about everything. She was really well prepared. She had a rucksack with her; an old smelly thing. Probably her dad's for tramping the hills. Agnes, all proud, told me how she'd got up early that morning and filled it with everything we might need in 1914.

"Like Irn Bru?" I said with a laugh. "Or bandages?" I stopped laughing, hoping we wouldn't need bandages.

"Bandages, definitely, and a torch and chocolate, and paper and pen and," she giggled, "toilet paper, and a book to read, my diary of course, because I will want to take notes, and my old teddy bear and a hair brush, and an old dress and—"

"Great," I interrupted her, "anyway, if we're going to do this, we better do it." I chewed my lip and shrugged. "Of course, we don't have to."

"Oh, but we do." Agnes was concentrating. "The earth is in place," she announced, "and the candle is lit."

I smiled weakly.

"Ok, turn the glass globe so it reflects the sun and throws off rainbows," I said, trying to sound bossy. The glass globe hung from a branch. Agnes winked at me, reached up and gave it a push and, sure enough, the coloured rainbows started to flash. With the glass globe swinging, Agnes played an old tune on the tin whistle. Then we pressed our left hands one on top of the other. Because she was wearing the gold ring, she touched the bark of the yew tree and my hand pressed over hers. Behind us the bonfire was crackling. We had put a pan of water over the flames. "Let the steam rise up into the rainbows," I shouted. There was a wobble in my voice. I couldn't help it. And there was a sinking feeling in my stomach. I couldn't help that either. Will and Robbie were in the den. That was the deal. They were to look after things in 2014.

"It's going to work," Agnes said, with no wobble in her voice. She looked round at me, winked, then closed her eyes and started singing the haunting old song.

The sun was climbing the sky on the longest day of the year. We had earth, air, fire and water, rainbows, vapours, and the antique song. We had gold. We had the ancient yew tree. We had both done this before for Agatha Black. We were trusting. Believing. Wanting this to work. At least, Agnes was, and I was trying hard. Everything was in tune, wasn't it? We imagined the time we were going to. The start of the First World War. We were going to save the den. We had faith. Agnes did, that was for sure. Her face looked totally focussed. I was working hard to have faith. If I didn't I could end up stuck in some in-between time, hovering forever. I tried to stop thinking of everything that could go wrong. Agnes, who was still singing the old song, had her time-travel kit on her back. I was pushed up against that smelly old rucksack. I kept opening my eyes, even though they were supposed to be shut. I was so close to Agnes, I could smell her shampoo. I had this random thought that last night must have been their bath night. I imagined them trouping off with their bars of soap and towels. Then I thought about going to Paris, even though I was supposed to have my mind completely full of 1914. Do French people really eat frogs' legs? How do you say 'No thanks!' in French?

"See... you... in... 1914..." Agnes murmured.

Then she vanished.

And I was left, touching the old bark of the yew tree murmuring, "Non... non merci."

6

I blinked. Maybe this was 1914? I was expecting weird sensations. But I felt fine. I blinked again and stared at the bark of the yew tree. Maybe it was a walk in the park, this time-travel romp? Maybe there was nothing to it? I swung round, expecting to see folk in strange clothes cutting the grass with scythes and pruning the rose bushes and smoking pipes. And maybe a few soldiers marching about. Where was Agnes? I heard a crackling sound and glanced over my shoulder, hoping it might be her. But it was a twig crackling in the fire. The fire was still going, still making coloured vapours. It would be a big coincidence if a bonfire happened to be burning in this very spot one hundred years ago. I had to check. I bolted up the garden to the den. It looked exactly like normal. There was that old stone at the door that I had carved SAULS GANG into with a piece of flint. And the bulldozer was still parked up behind the wall. I was not in 1914. I hadn't time travelled. I'd pressed my hand on a tree and gone nowhere.

I hovered at the den door wondering how I was going to explain this. Hearing me, Will and Robbie looked up from fiddling with their phones. They were pretty calm about their pals' time travelling just outside.

"Back already?" Will asked.

I shook my head. "Na," I muttered, "not gone yet." I didn't want them to know that Agnes had travelled on her own. "Just need something." And I hurried back outside. Courage, that's what I needed. I leaned against the den.

I had to face it: Agnes had gone and I had not. She was in 1914, trying to save this den, and find out about the war while she was at it. And here I was, the great gang leader, in the plain old twenty-first century. What was she doing? Probably looking for me. She might need me, and I was a hundred years away! The old time-travel formula that I had discovered on the internet was right: you had to fully, one hundred per cent want this to happen. Sounds simple enough, so the old scientist had written, yet in reality almost impossible.

But leaning against the den, wringing my hands together, something in me changed. My reluctance vanished. I stepped forward. Agnes might really need me. After all, I *was* the gang leader. Maybe we wouldn't lose the den. I felt this excitement pulse through me. Agnes might get into trouble with the war. I had to help her. I stared at my fingers. If I was going to travel back in time and catch up with Agnes I needed gold.

Next thing I was speeding over the fields and down the lane. Mum was out with the twins. Dad was out in the taxi. I burst into the house, ran up the stairs two at a time then there I was, in my parent's bedroom and lifting the little box that contained Mum's wedding ring. Since having the twins she never wore it. Said her fingers were too swollen. Good thing for me. I told myself this was borrowing for a good cause. She wouldn't miss it, because I'd be back in no time. I slipped it onto my pinkie, turned and ran.

Panting like mad, I made it back to the den and down to the yew tree. The fire was getting low, but still going. I just needed to reach up and push the glass globe. It swung out, catching the sun's rays and flashing rainbows around. The water in the pan was still steaming, enough to make pale vapours. I had earth, water, fire and air. I had coloured vapours and gold. I stood by the tree and glanced down at a patch of moss. I placed my feet on this small cushion, as though that might make a difference, and with my hand pressed against the tree I started to sing. It didn't sound too bad even though I was making it up as I went along. And this time I had faith. I really, one hundred per cent wanted to travel back in time. I wanted to catch up with Agnes Brown.

Then I really did get a buzzing in my ears. I kept singing but my voice didn't sound like my voice. It sounded as though it was coming from a long way off. The ground under my feet felt soft, as if the moss was dissolving and I might slip. The gold ring on my pinkie was burning. The air seemed to turn to gale-force wind and it was scary but still I wanted to time travel… and the buzzing grew louder… and my throat felt squeezed… and I was spinning… or being sucked down a long dark windy tunnel. But still I wanted to go.

It was dark.

"Help!" I cried, but 'Help!' stuck in my mouth.

7

The rest, you could say, was history. I ended up in a broom cupboard begging for a wee maid to set me free. I kicked her bucket. She flung open the door and out I stumbled, blinking, my heart pounding. I pelted along a gloomy corridor with that same wee maid yelling how she was going to set the housekeeper on me.

I could see ahead that the corridor opened onto a hall under a big sweeping staircase. Would Agnes be somewhere in this house too? I wanted to call out her name, but couldn't risk anyone else here knowing where I was. The wee maid had gone, probably to get the giant housekeeper she'd talked about. I was running past closed doors towards the lighter hall ahead. I didn't know if it was day or night, winter or summer. Maybe it was 1914, maybe it wasn't. I didn't know what the Hun was. I didn't know anything.

Before the hall, the corridor widened a bit and there was a small high window in an alcove. I stopped, stretched onto my tiptoes and looked out.

Then I knew something. Out there was the garden of our den and in the middle stood the yew tree. That was our yew tree, and our garden! The garden looked much neater and more flowery and not an overgrown total wilderness, but it was still the same place. The yew tree was exactly the same. A shiver crept over my skin.

Seeing the yew tree, I remembered the feeling of pressing Mum's gold wedding ring against the bark. I glanced down, worried I might have lost the ring time travelling, but there it was, dangling on my pinkie. I pulled it off. It was bad enough that I had 'borrowed' it; it would be ultra-bad if I lost it in history. I stuffed it deep in my jeans pocket for safety.

Where now? Up the stairs maybe? The door behind me had initials on it:

I had been here before – in the future. Playing hide and seek. It had only been yesterday for me, I think, but already time was feeling too messy to be sure. I shuddered, remembering how the house was a ruin then, with craggy bits still standing – like this room. Different time, same place. I pushed open the door and looked in. There was the cast iron bath. But it wasn't rolled on its side like it had been last time I saw it. It was upright and had legs like claws. And the place wasn't thick with dust. The toilet wasn't cracked, and there was no gap in the ceiling.

I took a hesitant step towards the bath, thinking 'This is crazy.' But then I heard a giggle. I knew that giggle. This enormous relief flooded through me. Agnes lifted her head and peered out over the rim of the bath.

"What took you so long?" she asked, clambering out

and darting her eyes around the place like a stowaway. She smiled at me, lifted her 'be prepared for history' rucksack out of the bath and swung it onto her back. "Am I glad to see you, Saul. I thought I was going to have to do this alone."

I shrugged and smiled back. "I wouldn't let you do that, Agnes. I'm the gang leader, don't forget."

Agnes winked at me. "This is the house," she said, excitedly. "I would know that bath anywhere." She laughed and I slammed my finger to my lips, meaning, 'Shhhhhh!'

"We have come to the right place," she whispered. "It's so exciting, Saul. It actually worked: the earth and vapours and antique song and gold. I heard a buzzing and my head felt dizzy. It all went dark, then next thing I knew, I was in the bath. With a spider! Where did you end up?"

"In a broom cupboard," I whispered, and suddenly it all felt like a great joke.

"Oh, Saul, what an adventure! But do you think we're in 1914? Have we come to the right time?"

I thought about that wee maid's voice, little cap, apron, long black dress, her talk of shillings and spies. I was no expert on the history of fashion, or money, but I reckoned we were more or less back one hundred years. "I think so," I whispered, "I met a maid. She's tiny." Right then I heard more footsteps stomping along the corridor.

"She doesn't sound tiny," Agnes gasped.

I grabbed her arm and steered her towards a big open cupboard full of towels and bars of soap. "That's not her," I hissed. "We need to hide, fast!"

8

Smells! I had only been in history minutes and already I'd had enough for a lifetime: first tar and bleach, now overpowering soap, and they all made me feel sick. Plus, this was the second cupboard I'd been in and, like I said, I hadn't exactly been in the past long. I imagined the postcards I would send – they'd be black:

Hi guys,
This is a cupboard. Be glad you're not here.
Hang loose.
Saul. X
1914 – I think!

"Whoever it is they're heading this way," Agnes whispered in my ear. (The edge of a shelf was jammed into my other ear.) I didn't need Agnes to tell me that. I could hear

STOMP-STOMP-STOMP

marching right into that bathroom – and, inside the cupboard, my heart going

THUMP-THUMP-THUMP

"You seeing things again, Elsie Noble? Because if you are it's a box round the ears you deserve."

"No, it was a spy; honest, Mrs Buchan, it was. A right rude, ugly one too. You said yourself there was a war coming."

Agnes nudged me in the ribs. I could tell by the way she was shaking she was trying hard not to laugh.

"Folks speak of little else. War, war, war." Mrs Buchan sounded scarily close, like on the other side of the cupboard, and probably at least six feet tall.

"And he was in stranger clothes than any I ever saw. Honest, Mrs Buchan."

I bit my lip. What if I suddenly got the hiccups? Or if Agnes suddenly sneezed?

"If I was given a penny for every time you said 'Honest, Mrs Buchan,' I'd be rich. I'd not kow-tow and polish and mend and Lord knows what else. I'd not rise at six to try and make order in this house. Oh no, Elsie Noble. I'd be off. I'd wash my hands of service once and for all and stride out of this house."

"I'm not making it up, honest, Mrs Buchan. A big boy was in the broom cupboard, he was. Frightened the living daylights out of me." It sounded like wee Elsie was ready to burst into tears. What if she got all wet in the face and yanked open the cupboard to fetch a towel?

"Talking of brooms, you need to scrub down the back hallway. *Scrub*, mind, not slap a wet flannel around the floor. That's after you've given this tub a good scouring.

The Master complained he took his bath with a spider. Any more shoddy work, Elsie Noble, and you'll be out on your ear. Now look sharp, and for the love of God, lassie, carry a clean handkerchief with you. We can't have you coughing all over the place. I don't need to remind you we've an important guest arriving. Lord knows Gaunt reminds *me* of it ten times a day." At last, the giant housekeeper stomped off. All went quiet out there in the W.C.

Elsie had a wee coughing fit, then sighed and said, "There's nothing wrong with a spider." Agnes elbowed me in the ribs. Elsie carried on. "Just because you and me's little, folks think they can just squash us and step on us, but it's not right. I'll put you over by the washstand then I can get on. Looks like the Master's been in the bath with his riding boots all mucky. Thinks just because he's rich he can do as he likes." Agnes shifted slightly. By this time a towel was sticking in my face. The wee maid kept up her chatter with the spider. "Easy for muckle Mrs Buchan to say 'Clean this, clean that, scrub this, scrub that.' It's not her whit fetches the water, is it? If Frank didn't help lug it in for me I don't know what I'd do. And I am too tired by far to fetch water now."

Then it sounded like the maid clambered into the bath, the very bath Agnes had just clambered out of. Then, judging by the little puttering snores we could hear, she must have fallen fast asleep.

"Saul," Agnes whispered, "the title deeds are not tucked away under the towels."

Then I heard her turn the handle. "Time for us to make a run for it." She opened the cupboard door.

We tiptoed out of the bathroom, leaving wee Elsie snoring lightly in the bath. Out in the corridor I glanced up and down. Agnes was at my elbow pulling on her trusty rucksack.

"This is thrilling," she whispered.

Something told me the thrills hadn't even begun. A dead deer with huge antlers was stuck up on the wall of the hall with the sweeping staircase. The house looked totally different from when we were in it with Will and Robbie playing hide and seek. Agnes and I bolted along the gloomy corridor, pushed open a door at the end and came into another big open hallway with black and white tiles on the floor. There was nothing much in it, except a coat stand with a black coat hanging on it. It had a door to the outside. Agnes tried to open it. "It's locked." She looked about her in a fluster. "What now?"

"The back of the house," I said and we sped off the way we'd come along the corridor, our footsteps echoing on the stone floors. No sign of Elsie, or the huge housekeeper. The place was eerily empty. A few worn steps led down and the corridor got narrower. "Definitely the servant's quarters," Agnes whispered, panting. "I read how ladies and gentlemen use the front door and front rooms, and servants use the back." By this time we'd reached the end of the narrow, dark corridor. "This is a back door," Agnes whispered. All the time we were glancing over our shoulders like spies. "Let's get outside," she hissed in my ear, "find some tree to hide in, then we can work out a plan. Ok, Saul?"

I shrugged. "Ok, Agnes," I whispered. Then I pushed opened the back door and we ran out into the past.

9

We found ourselves in some kind of cobbled yard and didn't know which way to turn. There were stables and outhouses. I'd never seen them before; none of them survived into the future. Then I heard someone behind me, whistling. I swung round and crashed into this guy who stumbled over and fell on his back, crying out. A fountain of water flew into the air and landed over both of us. I yelled and spluttered and heard a clanging sound as something metal hit the stony ground behind me. I looked down at this stranger sprawled on the cobbles. He was a bit older than us, but looked helpless, his brown baggy clothes all dirty and wet. His cap lay at my feet. It was soaked too.

"You poor thing," said Agnes, and there she was, quick as a flash, down on her knees next to him. "Are you hurt?"

"Don't kill me," he whimpered. His eyes kept darting to me, like he was really scared of me.

"Of course we won't." Agnes patted his arm. "What a thought."

"I wis only helping her out. It's too much for her. Now I'll have to fetch more." He scrambled to sit up, brushing down his dusty brown jacket, then reached for the cap and wrung out the water. All the time he gazed quizzically at our clothes. He winced like he was in pain. and looked beyond us to where a tin mop-bucket was lying on its side. "Are you American?" he asked us, rubbing his knee. His trousers had ripped.

I shook my head, not sure how to go about explaining who we were or where we were from.

"We're from… near here," Agnes muttered, busy fumbling about in her rucksack. Next thing she whipped out the roll of toilet paper and a little bottle of something. "That knee looks pretty bad," she said, pouring a few drops of whatever stinging stuff was in the bottle onto a wad of toilet paper. "Here," she said, getting ready to dab it onto his grazed knee, "this will clean it. Make sure there's no infection. Oh dear, you're bleeding. We are very sorry." She glanced meaningfully up at me.

"Yeah, really sorry. I didn't see you," I mumbled.

The boy on the ground gazed at us, wide-eyed and stunned, like we had dropped from the moon. I glanced down at my wet jeans and trainers and baggy skateboarding T-shirt. Agnes had on cut-off jeans and a bright yellow T-shirt. We didn't look that bad.

"Ow," he whimpered. No wonder – I could smell TCP.

"Would you like a painkiller?" Agnes asked, and that really freaked him out. I guess they might not have the word 'painkiller' in 1914. Maybe Calpol hadn't been invented yet. He dropped his wet cap, jumped to his feet, made a lunge for a dented tin mop-bucket behind us, and bolted off between two of the outbuildings. As he ran, I saw the soles of his boots were coming away. "Please, don't worry," Agnes called after him, "I didn't mean…"

But he was off, him and his clanging bucket and his broken boots. His cap was lying on the cobbled ground. I bent down and picked it up. "It might come in handy," Agnes said, stuffing her first-aid kit hastily back into the rucksack. She glanced about like she expected other servant boys to come crashing into us. But all was quiet again. The poor guy had disappeared.

Agnes looked me up and down then examined her knee-length jeans. I knew she was really proud of these shorts. She had cut them herself and fringed them around the knee, and even put in a few more rips and things. But next to the poor guy in the brown jacket, our clothes definitely looked out of place. "You're going to have to find something more old fashioned to wear," she whispered, rummaging about in her rucksack. "You should have thought of that. I brought something." Then she shook out this piece of brown material that looked like a baggy sack. Next thing she pulled it on. "I made a dress," she whispered, tugging it down. All of a sudden, Agnes Brown looked the part. "Pretty awful, eh?" She grinned. It was. But she did look right. She had even done something to curl her hair. In all the rush I hadn't noticed.

"Nice historic hair, Agnes," I said.

"Thanks," she said, shaking it about.

A bell rang inside the house. "We need to get out of here," I said, and we ran over the cobbles the opposite direction from where the guy had gone, round the stables, into the garden and over the grass. My jeans were wet and sticking to me, but it felt good to be back in our garden, even though it was different. The grass was all smooth and freshly mown, no tussocks, no bare patches. We found a tree. I think it was the oak tree we often climbed in 2014, only not as big. Agnes was up it in a flash, even with the bulky rucksack on her back. I wanted to check out the den but this didn't seem like the moment. I heaved myself up onto a thick branch after her.

Agnes had found a good sitting place and I squeezed in next to her. Up in the safety of the tree she wedged the rucksack between two branches. "Good thing I brought some chocolate," she announced, unwrapping a huge bar.

She was right about that. This was the kind of thing we would do in the gang: hang out in trees and munch on chocolate. It felt kind of comfortable up there. We polished the chocolate off pretty fast.

"How much have you got in there, Curly?" I asked her, picturing a whole sweetie shop in her rucksack.

"That was it, Soggy," she replied, with a smile. "Starvation ahead." Then I laughed. My jeans were damp, and a bit of branch was poking into my ribs, but it's amazing what half a bar of chocolate can do for your mood. I was actually starting to feel excited about being in the past. And there was something magical about Agnes's rucksack, like everything we needed would miraculously come out of it.

As if on cue she said, "I've made a plan," and fished her diary out. She opened it but didn't actually read it.

She obviously knew her plan off by heart. "First: find out where we are." She grinned across at me, her eyes shining in the flickering sunlight that was straying in through the leaves. "We got that right, didn't we Saul, because this is our garden, the garden of the den! And that's the big house. We did it! High five!" And we smacked our palms together.

"Step two, find out the date. I reckon we got that right too."

"More or less," I said and reeled off the clues so far. "Servants. Maids and stable boys. I mean, he looked like a stable boy. And horses. Spies. Enemies. Oh, and a shilling. I'm sure the wee maid mentioned a shilling. And how the war is coming."

Me and Agnes were feeling well pleased with ourselves. "Step three," she went on, "find the deeds of the old house."

For the first time, I really thought about saving our den – really pictured us going back to Will and Robbie and holding up the title deeds, shouting "We've got it; they can't bulldoze the den! We've saved it!" I felt the triumph of it. Agnes had been right: if we could do that, it was worth all the risks. Now we were back in 1914, we had to find these documents. Where could we start?

Agnes tapped her nose, like she did when she was working something out. "I've been thinking that it's probably too dangerous to try and search inside the big house. That housekeeper seems pretty scary. And the wee maid is not very pleasant either."

"Tell me about it! And what about Gaunt? The big master? He sounds bad news."

"Totally."

I was relieved I wasn't expected to break into the big house and rummage through all the rooms and cellars. I'd probably end up in jail and never get home!

"There are bound to be folk in town who know about this place," Agnes said. "We should head there and find out all we can. But," she looked at me through the leafy branches, "you need to dress more 1914, Saul. We're going to get all kinds of strange reactions with you looking so twenty-first century." She frowned, then her eyes lit up. "I know! Why don't you use that black cape thing we saw in the hall on the coat stand? Get that, then we'll head into town and find out all we can about Mr Hogg. He's the man my gran said owned this house. He is some distant relative of mine. Gran said I've got a great-great-great-great aunt called Jean who knows the truth. All we have to do is find her." Agnes lifted her rucksack. She was getting ready to climb down the tree. "Borrow that cape, Saul, then we'll go."

"Steal, you mean?" I clambered down after her. Agnes plus rucksack jumped down and landed softly on the grass. I followed. We glanced around nervously, but it all seemed very quiet. As we hurried up the garden I was picturing myself in a black cape. What a vision! I wanted to laugh out loud. Normally I wouldn't be seen dead in a black cape. But this wasn't normally.

When we neared the house we hid behind trees, checking the coast was clear. It was. No horse. No carriage. Not even a wisp of smoke curling from one of the high chimneys. I imagined little Elsie and the housekeeper and the stable boy, or whatever he was, tucked away somewhere in that big house. Maybe Mr Gaunt, or whoever he was, was off shooting hares.

"All you have to do," Agnes whispered, cutting in on my thoughts, "is open that window without a sound, slip in, grab the cloak and nip out. I'll wait for you under the window to check no one appears. Now go!" Feeling like a real thief, I climbed in through the open window, and belted across the empty hall to the coat stand.

"Oi!" I froze halfway across the black and white tiles, and looked up the flight of stairs. There was little Elsie standing on the landing, glaring down at me. This time she had a broom in both her hands, like one of those 'Halt! Who goes there?' soldiers. Her wee face was red and fierce looking. She stamped her foot. "Not having no robbers here!" she shouted. "Now get out, or there's going to be trouble. You hear?"

"This isn't what it looks like," I shouted back, as I sidestepped towards the coat stand.

"Mrs Buchan!" she roared and banged the broom on the floor.

I made a dive for the coat stand, yanked at the cape and pulled it off the hook. The stand overturned and crashed to the ground.

"STOP, THIEF!" Elsie yelled. The heavy bundle of the cloak fell into my arms. I turned and ran, my heart hammering like a war drum.

10

I wriggled through the open window with the bulky coat in my arms. Agnes was under the window, hiding in the shadows.

"The height of fashion," she whispered. "Ok Saul, time to go to town!"

The two of us pounded up the garden, Elsie still shrieking behind us. We knew the garden well, and were soon out of sight of the house. No one was coming after us. We darted round behind the den, and stopped there, hidden. My heart was pounding.

There was no more shrieking. We were going to have to make ourselves scarce, but we were hiding behind our den! I so wanted to go in and see what it was like in 1914. By the way Agnes was staring at it, so did she.

"Just a quick peek," I whispered. I shot a glance back up the garden. Still no movement.

Agnes lowered her rucksack. I dropped the stolen cape over it and we sidled round the hut. "What if someone's in here?" We were both pressed up against the hut, trying not to make a sound. "Budge over," she whispered, nudging me, and she lent sideways to peer in through the window. "Oh," she gasped, "it's lovely."

She was right. It was so tidy inside. No one was

there. There was a bed, a little table and a chair. A jar of roses stood on the table beside a pile of books. Leaning up against one wall of the room was a row of garden tools.

"YOU ARE NEARER GOD IN A GARDEN THAN ANYWHERE ELSE ON EARTH"

whispered Agnes, reading a piece of stitching on the wall above the bed. "How cute."

"Someone lives here," I said.

Agnes elbowed me. "There's someone over there," she whispered, "where we usually play. Look!" She was right. Where we were used to seeing our grassy mucking-about space there was a big vegetable garden with rows and rows of green stuff. And there was someone in it, hunched over. "Probably the gardener. I think he's picking carrots," Agnes whispered. Thankfully he was so focussed on his carrots he didn't turn round.

We hurried back to where we'd left our stuff, grabbed it and pelted for the hole in the hedge. By habit, we were going our usual way. But the hole in the hedge wasn't there. And the hole in the wall wasn't there either. There was no way we could wriggle through a thick hedge then scale a high wall. And we had to get out of this garden before Elsie rounded up the servants to search for us. It felt a shame to leave the den, but it wasn't ours yet, and if we didn't get a move on it wouldn't be ours ever again.

"I saw a gate," Agnes said, "we can get out that way. Let's go."

So away we ran, down the long garden, darting from

tree to tree. Now we had a gardener to avoid as well as a maid, a stable boy and a housekeeper. He might pelt carrots at us. And what about the dreaded master who might turn up at any moment? He might lock us in the broom cupboard, and whack us with a stick. He might cart us off to a home for misbehaving children. When we reached the farthest end of the garden, we were out of breath and a bit panicked.

"There!" Agnes hissed, pointing to tall black iron gates. These didn't survive into the future. But right now they were ahead of us, closed, and very high. Agnes stepped boldly out onto the gravel drive to try the big black iron latch. The gates were locked. I tried too but they wouldn't budge.

I groaned.

"We'll have to climb over," Agnes said, like it would be easy-peasy. Did she not notice these gates were way higher than the climbing wall at school? And there were no foot grips. Was she mad? "We can grab one of the iron rails and go up hand over hand. Unless," she said, "you've got any better suggestions?"

I could hear distant drumming. I tugged Agnes's arm and pulled her behind one of the thick bushes that grew along the wall on either side of the high gates. I squatted down and shoved the huge black cape thing over us. The drumming came closer.

"I think that's a horse," I mumbled. Agnes put her ear to the ground then lifted her head, giving me the thumbs up. "Don't move," I whispered. Our disguise, I thought, was pretty good. We were squeezed in the middle of a bush with a black cape over us. A sniffing dog would find us but otherwise we'd be safe. The hooves came nearer.

If horses and people were coming to the house, someone would open the gates. An escape plan took shape in my head. A better one than trying to scale the high gates. "Soon as these huge gates open, get ready to run." I hissed. "The second they're in, we'll nip out!"

"Steady there, steady! Whoa! Steady now!" A man's voice rang out. At the same time a horse neighed loudly. "Noble!" the man roared, and next minute I could hear footsteps running. By the funny clacking noise, I knew it was the stable boy in his broken boots.

"Coming, sir," he shouted. "Be there in a minute, sir." Then a jangling noise, a key clicked, the gate creaked, a horse whinnied.

"Why so slow, Noble? Sleeping on the job again, eh? I've been waiting a full five minutes to enter my own estate," the man bellowed. This, I guessed, was Gaunt.

If we were going to get out we'd have to make a run for it, now. I pulled the cape down and peered out. The man who must be Gaunt was riding his horse through the gate.

I pulled the cape off. "Run!" I hissed.

11

Agnes was on her feet in a second. We stepped out from our hiding place behind the bush and there we were, in the open air. But my plan was perfect. Gaunt was heading towards the house, already past us. The stable boy was holding the open gate. He swung round, surprised, when he heard us.

"Let us out, please?" Agnes whispered. Before he could decide, we tore through. Agnes spun round and waved to him. "Thanks!" she called, then we turned and ran.

We knew our way. Over a wall, across a farmer's field. That hadn't changed. We didn't stop running until we reached the top of the lane that wound down into the town centre.

There, we leaned back against a wall, panting and bright red in the face. I tried on the cape, throwing it around my shoulders. I looked ridiculous. I knew I would. And my trainers definitely gave the game away. Agnes had lost a flip-flop in the field so she threw the other one away. With her baggy old brown dress, curly hair and bare feet, she did look pretty historical.

"I hope that poor boy is ok," she said. Then she looked down at my feet and frowned.

"What's up?" I grinned at her. We had escaped. We were in Peebles. No one had come after us! I couldn't wait to do a bit of exploring now. This was it. The adventure could begin.

"You're going to have to take your trainers off," she said. "Hide them. Trainers haven't been invented yet, especially ones with a fluro stripe. You'll freak people out."

'What about my feet?' I wanted to say, but I knew she was right. I took them off, wondering where I could hide them. I liked these trainers. They cost a lot of money. Mum would be fuming if I lost them.

"Under that pile of logs," Agnes suggested, pointing to a neat stack outside a house in the lane. So I carefully dislodged one log from low down in the pile, slid the trainers in behind it, then slipped the log back in. I tried to memorise which log. Agnes was yanking at my cape. "Come on," she said, "let's go." And she was off. This time it was me following her. She still had her rucksack on, bobbing up and down on her back. She thought it blended in fine. It was old fashioned, but not that old fashioned.

The cape flapped about and was really awkward to run in. "If Will and Robbie could see me now," I thought, and started laughing. Once I started I couldn't stop. Try running and laughing at the same time. And try running barefoot when you're not used to it. Because just then I stood in a big pile of horse poo. That stopped me laughing. I yelled. It was gross. And it was everywhere. Looking up I saw dollops of horse poo all up and down the road. You don't get that on this lane in the twenty-first century. I shook my foot about, as if that would do any good.

"Look at the daft laddie," somebody shouted. Next thing people were gathering around me. Barefoot kids, a couple of skinny dogs, and an old man with a grizzly beard. They were all staring at me. I felt stupid with a mucky foot but held my head up, like I didn't care.

"Let's go and wash it off in the river," said Agnes. She actually blended in well with the other ragged barefoot kids standing about. Except maybe for the rucksack. We headed down the cobbled wynd to the river, plonked ourselves down on the bank and I dunked my dirty foot into the water. That felt good. I dipped my other foot in too. Agnes took off her rucksack and did the same.

We sat there for a while, with the river running past and people walking by on the other side. It was a nice day. The kids looked ragged and the boys wore long brown or grey shorts and baggy shirts. The girls had on dresses and flouncy aprons. They mostly had bare feet too. They had long hair, most of the girls, curly, like Agnes, or in plaits with huge floppy ribbons. Some had wide-brimmed hats on.

"I think we got it right, Saul," Agnes said. "I do believe it's 1914."

"So, where are all the soldiers?"

"The war hasn't started yet, silly!" she said, and poked me in the ribs.

The cool water tickled my toes. 1914 was ok. The river was the same. Peebles felt like the town I knew, just with more sheep about and horses. And horse poo in the streets. There were more children too. The children were all out, playing and running about, without any parents with them, even little ones. The bells on the church clock rang out, sounding just like they do in the twenty-first century.

A rowing boat came down the river. There were three people in it, all dressed up with straw hats on, lazily trailing their hands in the water over the side of the boat. It looked like a painting. Everything felt so peaceful. Maybe 1914 was actually better than the future?

"Too bad Peebles doesn't have rowing boats on the river in the twenty-first century," I said. "I like it here."

Agnes nodded, pulled a small towel from her bag, dried her feet then flung the towel to me. "So, great traveller through time," she said with a wink, "let's keep walking. We can check out the town, maybe try and find my great-great-great-great auntie Jean? At least, Gran thinks she's called Jean. If she's not Jean, she's Joan." Agnes swung her bag onto her back and grinned at me.

I jumped to my now really clean feet and we walked on. The cape was a serious nuisance. And I looked stupid in it. It covered my clothes from the future, but I didn't look like the other boys around us. What I really needed was some baggy shorts like they had on. If we had some money, we could probably buy a pair. I had two pounds in my pocket but no one in 1914 would recognise the coins. Pound coins hadn't been invented yet. And these ones had dates on them that would blow everyone's mind. So they were no use at all.

But they gave me the idea how we could earn some 1914 coins.

"You're a good singer, Agnes." I said.

She cocked her head to the side. "Meaning?"

"We could give history a pop song. Bit of Adele maybe. Or The Who – they're old fashioned. Or you could sing the Robert Burns song you like "For a' that and a' that" I chanted. "We could get some 1914 money and use it for clothes, and maybe something to eat. We can't go on stealing. Then we really will get locked up and be stuck here forever."

Back in our time, Agnes's dad played the fiddle on Peebles High Street. He could make about £50 on a good day. Agnes knew all about busking. "Well, Saul," she said, "if I am going to stand on the street corner and sing, you've got to join in. Promise?"

There is totally no way I would normally promise to stand on the street corner and sing. But we weren't in our time, so I did!

12

The Peebles streets hadn't changed much, so I had the feeling that I knew my way about, kind of. I was keeping my eyes glued to the ground not wanting to go stepping into horse dung again. Agnes, skipping along beside me, kept up a running commentary.

"Like I expected, hardly any cars. Horses, of course. Big plodding horses, Clydesdales mostly, pulling carts and carriages. No sign of a war though," she went on, lowering her voice. "No posters up saying

YOUR COUNTRY NEEDS

YOU!

– not yet!" By this time we had reached Peebles High Street and were walking along the pavement. Agnes said she was pretty certain horses weren't allowed on the pavement, so I could relax.

"Nice car," Agnes said, admiringly. She was right. It was slowly chugging along at about 5 miles an hour. The driver was pressing one of those rubber horn things, and waving like he was the king. The car was yellow and didn't have a top. It looked more like a posh horse carriage than an actual car. The folks on the street all flocked to see it. People waved to the driver. Some took off their caps and waved them in the air. "Maybe he's famous, like a celebrity," Agnes whispered, as the car pulled up close to us. With more toots on the horn and a wheezing sigh on the brakes, the famous yellow car stopped. A small crowd gathered and some people reached out to touch the paintwork.

The driver, who was dressed in tweed knee-length trousers and a fancy jacket with a yellow scarf around his neck, was clambering down. He was telling the crowd to keep their grubby little paws off his spanking new motorised car.

Next to us an old man with a walking stick was shaking his head and talking away to whoever would listen. "Aye, it's young Anderson. I mind well when the Andersons had not much more than a horse and a few sheep to their name. Then this one's father came back from Glasgow and built the cotton mill. Now they live in a great house like a castle. And look, here's young Anderson gone and bought a fancy new motor, like some lord of the manor. I remember when if you were born to a bit of land, you lived on it and died on it. But it's all change now. Andersons acting like lords and ladies, and driving round in motors. Who'd a thought of it."

Agnes wasn't distracted by the old man. She nudged me. I knew what was coming. Her dad was always saying how you had to take advantage of crowds. "Remember," she hissed, rummaging in her rucksack, "join in!" She pulled out the stable boy's cap and shoved it into my hands. I felt a proper fool standing there begging, especially with a damp cap, but Agnes burst out singing.

♪♪ *"By yon bonnie banks and by yon bonnie braes..."* ♪♪

The crowd turned their gaze from the yellow car to the singers on the street. Us! Agnes sounded good. She was used to busking, because of her dad, and you could tell she came from a family where they sang a lot. Her voice rang out all clear, filling the street.

I felt my cheeks turn beetroot. I didn't even know the words. How was I supposed to join in? So I hummed the tune. I had to do something.

"I like a good song," the driver of the car announced, his voice booming and his big moustache wriggling up and down. Things were going to plan. He plunged his hand into his jacket pocket, brought out a coin and placed it into my cap.

I mumbled "Thank you," and Agnes kept singing.

♪♪ *"So you'll tak the high road and I'll tak the low road..."* ♪♪

A few folk in the crowd clapped along with great gusto.

♪♪ *"And I'll be in Scotland afore ye..."* ♪♪

Passers by stopped to listen. There was one woman in the crowd who, I noticed, was humming along to Agnes's tune. I couldn't help staring at her. She had long thick grey hair with a shawl wrapped around her shoulders and a flowing dark green skirt on. Her eyes seemed to match the green of her skirt. She kept smiling. There was a white flower in her hair.

I actually knew the next bit so I joined in.

"For me and my true love will never meet again, on the bonnie, bonnie banks of Loch Lomond."

I had heard Runrig singing this song. My dad loved Runrig. He had all these old CDs. I felt a pang of homesickness, thinking about my dad. Was time passing there without me? Were they missing me? What if Will was wrong? Would the police be out looking for us? Would the den be bulldozed already?

I was so caught up thinking about home I didn't see the commotion in the crowd. Agnes obviously didn't either. She had already plunged into the next song –

"Robin was a rovin' boy, rantin' rovin' Robin…"

– quite a few people were now singing along, and we had a handful of coins jingling in the cap. Then the crowd was pushed aside. I saw that the smiling woman with the white flower in her hair was almost knocked over. I thought a fight had broken out. A big man stomped through the crowd and glared at me. And there, by his side, was little Elsie. She was pointing straight at me.

"That's him!" she shouted. "I swear on my poor dead mother's grave. That's him! And that's Frank's cap!"

"And that," the big man roared, "is my best rain cape! Dirty little thief. Grab him!"

13

I dropped the cap and the coins rattled on the ground. Agnes screamed. The big man lurched towards me. I felt his strong grip around my wrist. Elsie was wagging her finger at me and yelling, "Told you, eh? Nobody gets to make a fool of poor Elsie. Nobody gets to kick my bucket and get away with it." She snatched the cap from the ground. I think she snatched the coins too. "I told you, didn't I? You'd pay for it. Didn't I tell yer? Eh?"

The big man yanked the cape off me and I stood there in my jeans and skateboarding T-shirt. The crowd gasped. Some people stepped back. I looked around frantically for Agnes. You'd think I was stark naked the way they gaped at me, pop-eyed. And little Elsie was seriously annoying me. She kept on with her, "Eh? Eh? Eh?" I wanted to tell her to shut up. I wanted to tell them I wasn't a real thief. I didn't even want the cap or the cape. But I couldn't get any words to come out.

"Boys have had a finger chopped off for less," roared the driver of the yellow car. I heard this whimper come out of my throat.

"Don't talk nonsense," someone shouted. It was the woman with the white flower.

"If anyone talks nonsense around here," bellowed the man who had me by the wrist, "it's you, Jean." He glared at the woman who glared right back at him. Then he turned to the crowd, still grabbing hold of me. "House breaking is a right serious offence, is it not? And stealing my cape to boot. I'll have yea, laddie."

"He was in the broom cupboard," Elsie told the crowd, her thin arms thrust on her hips. "Kicked my bucket. I got the fright o' my little life. I thought he was the enemy." I got a mighty boo out of the crowd for that. I didn't know where to look. "Aye, or a ghost," she went on, and the crowd laughed. "Just cause I'm half-pint size doesnae mean he can make a fool out of me." The crowd were booing and shaking their fists at me.

"Throw him in jail," somebody yelled.

"Actually," the big man was eyeing me up and down, "you're a strapping laddie."

His bushy eyebrows lifted, like he'd just had a great idea. "Lugging coal up and down the flights of stairs is too much for little Elsie here and her brother has got the horses to see to. I could do with more staff. Especially at the moment."

"Aye! Quite right," Elsie piped up. "Give him hard labour!"

"Splendid idea," the big man replied, and the crowd were nodding and laughing. I wriggled and squirmed but his fingers were wrapped tight around my wrist. I couldn't get away, and Agnes was nowhere to be seen. "You're coming home with me, dirty thief." I hoped wherever Agnes was, she heard him. "I'll make an honest man out of you. A few weeks work, I would say, is a fair price for trying to steal my best rain cape."

"You're just making young folk work for nothing, Gaunt." The woman with the flower, who had shouted out before, wasn't backing down.

My captor glared at her like she was dirt. She just glared straight back at him, then spat on the ground at his feet. I felt him tighten his grip. Tears welled up in my eyes. Then he marched me off, Elsie skipping about me like a yapping dog and that cursed black cape flung over his shoulder flapping like a mad crow.

My feet were cut and sore. We were heading up the lane. I knew the way. We were going back to the big house. I couldn't believe this was happening. "He's a common thief," the big man announced to the world, dragging me along like I was his naughty dog.

"Aye, a bloomin' common thief," echoed Elsie, who seemed to be having the time of her life. "He's getting hard labour," she shouted, "starting today!"

I was being hauled across the field towards the big house when I heard three whistles coming from up a tree. I felt a burst of hope. That was Agnes. She was following me.

The big iron gates were in sight. Elsie ran ahead and clanged a bell. A boy came running out with a bunch of keys. Right away I knew it was the same boy that I had knocked over, the one who had opened the gates before. He flashed me a look, then, as he swung open the gates, he winked at me. He only looked about thirteen. He kept nodding to the big man and saluting. "I've hired a new coal man," my captor announced, frogmarching me through the gates. "He's a dirty thief and there'll be no hobnobbing with him, you hear?"

The gate boy nodded his head and muttered, "Yes, sir."

The big man pushed me into the house and through a door, into a room lined with bookshelves. There was a big leather desk and a chair. It was hard to concentrate on what was happening because it was so weird to be back where I'd been with Will and Robbie and to remember the shelves all falling down and the books rotting. "Terms and conditions are these," the man began, like he was spitting out the words. He drummed his fingers on the table. "You work hard for me and in return I give you a roof over your thieving head, food and a blanket to lay your thieving head down on at night. Steal as much as a lump of sugar and it'll be rat-infested jail for you." He flashed me a threatening look. "Nobody, but nobody, makes a fool out of me. Do you understand?"

I nodded. I felt miserable.

"What's that in your pocket, thief?" he demanded. "Turn it out!" He'd seen the shape of the ring. With a heavy feeling inside, I pulled it out. "Where did you steal this?" he roared, swiping it. Things were going from very bad to worse. I'd never get home without that ring. And it was Mum's wedding ring. I couldn't speak. "This will be your bond," he said with a snarl, pocketing it. "If you break the terms and conditions, or if you try to run away, you forfeit the ring – it becomes mine. Do you understand?"

I nodded.

"Good," he said. Then he twirled the ends of his long moustache. "Welcome to Gaunt House. Gaunt's my name." He was practically stabbing himself in his puffed-up chest. "'The Master'" to you." Then, "Noble!" he bellowed.

I shuddered. What a roar!

"Right here, sir." The boy must have been standing at the ready behind the door.

Gaunt pointed to me, "Put him on fire duty, and if Mrs Buchan needs help he can lend a hand where required. He can be," he looked me up and down, "the lad o parts." He laughed at that and I shivered, imagining myself cut in lots of parts. "The chimneys are due a sweep too. He's to sleep in the bunker room next to the kitchen. I want this house ready soon. And I mean soon! The American guest is due any day."

"Yes, sir," said Noble, robot style. So far he hadn't even flicked his eyes towards me.

"He'll take his meals with you and Elsie. And watch him. He's a thief."

"Yes sir."

"Doesn't have a name. Call him Blackie! He'll be black soon enough, working with the fires. And tell Elsie to run up fitting articles of clothing. Nothing fancy. At least, not till the important guest arrives. Then we'll have to have him presentable looking."

"Yes, sir."

Gaunt nodded. We were dismissed.

I followed the boy called Noble down a narrow corridor. The stone floor was cold, which was alright for him, he didn't have bare feet. I wondered where

Agnes was. Still up a tree probably, planning my escape. She didn't know the terms and conditions. The only safe escape would be a fast one back to the future. My head was buzzing. My teeth were chattering. Noble stopped suddenly and I almost bumped into him. We had come to the end of the narrow passageway. He slipped a key in a lock and turned it, pushed open a creaking door and we stepped into a dimly lit and damp-smelling cupboard of a room.

"Welcome tae yer humble home," he said.

14

"Clean the grates." Noble was speaking to me. "Ash goes oot the back on the compost heap. Guid for the grass. Some fires hav'nae been swept for months. Once they're a' swept, black them and polish them. Then hoik the coal up. Set a' the fires. Dinnae drop coal dust. Dinnae get grubby fingerprints on the wa's."

I stared at him. I'm sure my jaw was falling open. It was like he was reciting a weird poem to his boots. I didn't understand anything. I felt like laughing and saying, 'Ok, joke over. Let's go out on our bikes. Let's go and see a movie. Let's stuff our faces with popcorn and fizzy drinks then play the Xbox.' But he just kept going.

"Dinnae dae onything tae fash sister Elsie. She's no been well. Dinnae dae onything tae fash the housekeeper. She's got a right short temper on her. The gardener keeps his own company. And for God's sake, dinnae look the wrong way at Gaunt. Dinnae dae onything against the…" then he stopped in his flow and actually looked at me, "terms an' conditions." Then he looked back at the floor.

My mind raced. Robbie's mum had a wood-burning stove. That was a fire. Will's granny had a coal fire. He said it kept her fit, cleaning it every day. He said sometimes the wind blew down the chimney and smoke blew into the house. You could buy plastic sacks of coal from the garage. But it was summer now. What were they doing having fires in the summer time? Though it was kind of chilly and damp in that huge house. 'Dinnae fash...' Dad said that sometimes. It meant 'Don't annoy...' or something like that. My head hurt. I shivered. My knees were shaking. I couldn't hold myself up. I heard this whimpering noise, and realised it was coming from me. The room was spinning. I was going to fall...

Noble was towering over me.

"Tea." His lips were moving. "Cup o' tea fir yea, Blackie." Who was Blackie? "A good cup o' tea. That'll see ye right."

I was in a heap on the floor. Maybe I fainted. My head was still spinning. I felt sick. I couldn't move. Make this end. Make it all a bad dream.

"Aye," I heard him mumble, "a wee bit sugar in it and ye'll be right as rain." I heard the teaspoon clink. "Aye, Gaunt pits the fear o' God in folks." There he was with a cup in his hand. "Proper good stewed tea!"

I didn't even like tea. 'Give me Irn Bru,' I wanted to yell, but I groaned and hoisted myself up onto my elbows. Then I managed to sit up. What I liked and didn't like counted for nothing. Irn Bru probably wasn't invented yet. "Thanks," I mumbled, and took the cup.

"Wet yer whistle on that, Blackie," he said.

It was bitter, sweet and overpowering. But it tasted good, in a painful way. I drank the whole cup, and thought 'wet yer whistle' – I must remember that.

I thought how I'd tell Will and Robbie to wet their whistles. Even though I was in dire straits, I couldn't stop a smile creeping over my face.

"What did I tell yea?" said Noble with a funny wee clap of his hands, "there's nothing like a guid cup o tea to pit the world to rights. Many's the time I'm that tired I could lie mysel down and die, and what pits me to rights? Aye, you've guessed it, Blackie; a cup o' tea."

I nodded. What else could I do? I had this sinking feeling that this was no dream. I was still sitting on the stone floor, dazed, with the empty cup in my hand. I knew if I stood up I would fall. Noble bent down and took the empty cup from me.

"Run away frae the poor house, did ye?" Then he shook his head in pity. "Right queer-looking clothing they give yea. Wasn't like that in my day, but nae doot things have changed. If you don't mind me saying, Blackie, you look like a thief in they clothes."

This strangled little laugh burst out of my throat. If he had any idea how much these jeans had cost Mum, he wouldn't be shaking his head and feeling sorry for me. And if he had any idea what a frump he looked. He was dressed like an old man, but he was probably not much older than me.

"We'll have you kitted out and looking spic and span in no time," he said, flicking a crumb from his baggy jacket. "Gaunt has a finger in a' manner o' pies. The poor house is one o' his pies, if yea get ma drift." I didn't. But it was beginning to dawn on me that Noble was ok. If he took off the mad clothes he would look pretty cool. "What I mean tae say, is," he bent closer to me and lowered his voice, "they're not going to come here beating the door down for yea." He sighed. "They didn't bother coming after me and my sister Elsie."

I felt like telling him how I wasn't from the poor house, whatever that was. I wanted to tell him the whole time travel story. I wanted him to know I wasn't that poor and I was actually going to go on the school trip to France. My mouth fell open but no words came.

"His majesty, Mr Gaunt, is dining out today," he said, yawning. "He willna be back for a guid couple o' hours. Sometimes he goes off for days. God alone kens where." Poor guy looked exhausted. He had dark patches under his eyes and his skin was pale like he hardly ever saw the sun. He locked the door and stuffed the huge bunch of keys into an inside pocket of his jacket. "You and me can have a wee kip for an hour or so. His majesty will be none the wiser and Mrs Buchan's doon the toon buying linen to make bed sheets. And no doubt she'll spend a good hour gossiping. She's never in any hurry tae get back here."

And unbelievably, he sat down, stretched out on the cold stone floor, took off his too-small cap and placed it carefully down next to him, rolled onto his side, folded his hands under his cheek, closed his eyes, mumbled, "Good night, Blackie," and went to sleep.

"My name's Saul," I said, but he was snoring by then so I don't think he heard.

15

Agnes

I had the strangest feeling while I was singing on the street. It was like the jostling crowd fell away and there was only one person there listening. I felt certain I was staring into the green, sparkling eyes of my very own great-great-great-great aunt. Then that big man who grabbed Saul called her 'Jean'. It must be her. But I couldn't stop and try to talk to her, or even thank her for standing up to the man. I had to follow Saul when he was dragged away. Now I was in a big tree outside the garden wall of the big house. What was going on in there? What could I do to help Saul? I took out my diary and my pencil. When there's no one to talk to it is a relief to talk to my diary.

Dear diary
It is 1914. I now know for sure it is the 2nd August 1914. Britain declares war on Germany in two days time. I happen to know that. Some people here might guess it

is coming, but from what I could see in the town high street, most folk don't. At least, they're not expecting anything bad is about to happen. They seem quite happy going about their business.

We didn't get to have a really good look around before that funny little servant girl found poor Saul. By the way she was coughing I think her days are numbered, which makes me feel sorry for her, even though she is annoying. Anyway, the war is coming and lots of these people's days are numbered, though of course they don't know it. I saw a calendar in the butcher's shop window. It was called an Almanac and it said the date, which is how I know. And Saul is prisoner. And I am like a bird in a tree. These are my options:

1. Go back into town and try to find my great-great-great-great aunt. She looks the kind of person who might help us out.
2. Walk boldly up to the back door of the big house, ring the bell and ask for a job. If I managed to get one, Saul and I would both be in there together.
3. Go back to town and find out what I can about this house.

Plan number 3 feels like the best thing to do, at least for starters. I don't know what time it is.

Somewhere in the afternoon, I think. Oh diary, I hope so much that Saul is ok. This whole thing was my idea. I know I forced him into it, kind of. I just get so excited about doing important things. Now I wonder what is happening to him? I hope he gets good food to eat. I hope they don't make him work too hard, because I don't think he is used to it, like I am. But he's the gang leader and clever. He will be ok, I think.

I will stop writing now because I have reached the bottom of this page.

I wondered about the rucksack. People did look at it funny so I decided to leave it hidden in this tree. I parted the branches to check the coast was clear, then jumped down, and headed back over the field. Half the houses I know in Peebles are not built yet. It looks a smaller place. And lots of the trees I know haven't grown yet. When I walked over the bridge I noticed it had shrunk. It was narrower and I had to get out of the way when a horse and cart clip-clopped and rumbled past. I couldn't help but stand and stare. Especially when I saw there was a pile of bones heaped onto the back of the cart. The hills were the same. The steeples were the same. But the people walked slower and the women were wearing long skirts. The mills down by the river puffed out thick smoke from their chimneys. This is my town, I kept telling myself. This is Peebles in the past.

I saw strange old-fashioned shops called 'drapers' and 'glovers', a rag store and a temperance hotel.

(I've read about temperance. It's people not getting drunk.) I tried not to look too astonished at everything because I needed to fit in. There were sheep and cows, even as close in as the bank of the river. I saw folk going about their business. Most of them looked like they worked in the mills. The men wore flat cloth caps and sometimes they doffed them to me and said "good day". Which I thought was very polite and friendly. I also noticed how a few men whistled as they walked along the street. I never heard anyone in the twenty-first century whistle tunes on the street. There was a woman with a cart full of fish, she was crying out, "Herring, caller herring." There were young children playing marbles and hopscotch. Their word for hopscotch was 'peevers.'

Down on the green I could see some women hanging out washing and chatting together. Maybe I could find some things out by talking to them? The women had big baskets of washing and were pegging-up sheets and even big baggy pants for all the town to see. My gran would call a sunny and breezy day like this "a good drying day". I remembered the woman with the white flower and the green skirt. Her hair had been all tumbling down; these women all wore their hair tucked up in buns or hidden under scarves. My great-great-great-great aunt Jean – if it *was* her – wasn't here.

The women were practically shouting at each other to be heard across the green. "It'll no come to that," one woman called out, pegging up a flapping white sheet. "If it does, our boys will sort them out, no question about it."

"Aye, 'Rule Britannia' maybe, but if I don't get this washing pegged up soon, I'll be late making his dinner and you ken whit he's like if his dinner's no on the table at noon. *Then* there'll be a war!"

"Because he wouldna lift a hand tae mak it himself now, would he?"

A few of the women chuckled at that. I was hovering nearby, looking interested in daisies and picking a few. "Instead of making daisy chains, lassie," someone shouted, "you could be passing up these wooden pegs to me."

I swung round, realising she was talking to me. Another woman lowered her basket and studied me. "You should by rights be in the school."

"Oh, rights, is it?" another one said. "And where was rights when I was scullery maid at the age of twelve, eh?"

Another woman hooted with laughter. "That was a long while, back Jessie Linton, when boys went up chimneys. You're no spring chicken and, let me remind you, times have changed."

"They're going to change even more," I blurted out, then smacked my hand over my mouth. Silly me. But I wanted to let them know. I wanted them to know they would lose sons and husbands and grandsons in the muddy trenches.

But they just laughed. "Over here wee missy and huld this peg basket. Make yourself useful."

I slipped the daisy chain round my neck then went

over and held the peg bag. It was easy to chat to these women and soon I was asking them about the big house up the lane and beyond the field. "The one with the huge iron gates and the big wall all round it," I said, handing up giant wooden pegs. "Whatever happened to the old man who used to own it?"

"Ah now, him?" The women shook their heads. "Poor old John Hogg? I thought everybody hereabout kent the story of poor old John Hogg…"

My heart missed a beat actually hearing the name of John Hogg. So Gran was right! But I just kept passing the pegs. "Aye, lassie," said another woman, "and who are you anyway, that you don't know?"

"And who's your mother, eh?" They were closing in on me, with their scarves round their heads and their big bright faces. One of them had brown teeth.

A tear rolled down my face and I stared down at my bare feet on the grass. "She's dead."
One woman put a strong arm around my shoulder. "Don't cry pet. She'll be in a better place and Lord knows we'll all follow her there soon enough." Then with a damp hankie she wiped my face. "They don't tell you much up in that poor house, do they? Stop the tears, lassie, and I'll tell you about poor John Hogg."

16

"Wake up, Blackie."

"Mum," I said, mumbling, "I don't want to eat frog's legs. Tell them I don't want any."

"Get up, quick. He's here. I can hear him. Shift!"

"Where's Mum? What?" I blinked, and blinked again. I felt this huge disappointment crash inside me. I thought this was a bad dream. It wasn't. Noble was shaking me. He looked seriously worried. I felt so tired, but he was grabbing me and hoisting me up to my feet.

"Let's flee tae the coal shed," he said. "Pretend we've been there all this time. Me showing you the ropes." He flung open the back door, ran outside then beckoned wildly for me to follow.

I could hear Gaunt shouting at the other end of the house, calling for someone to take his horse and swearing about his servants and how lazy they were.

"Quick!" Noble hissed. He was already pelting across the backyard.

I ran, my bare feet jabbing over sharp stones. Trying hard not to yell out I followed him round the back of the house.

There were a few dilapidated stone outhouses. Noble shoved me into the dingiest-looking shed. I felt coal dust smother the back of my throat. "Right then, Blackie," Noble said, panting like mad as I was choking my head off, "this is the coal shed and here's where you fetch coal. This is a bucket and that over there's a shovel. Shovel as much coal into the bucket as you can and break your back hauling it up a hundred stairs. Any room on the first floor wi' a stick of furniture in it and a fireplace needs a fire. That's his majesty's quarters. First, clean oot the ash. Ye'll need another bucket for the ash. Then set the fire, then light it. And for God's sake, be quick about it! I'll open the back door. Go in that way." Then he turned and fled. Off to take the saddle off the horse probably.

"Matches?" I wailed to his flying ragged jacket. "What about matches?" Surely matches were invented? If I was expected to rub stones together, I'd never get as much as a spark. Thankfully Noble heard me. He stopped, pulled a small box from his pocket and hurled it to me. Phew! Matches did exist! I hurried back into the gloomy coal shed, grabbed the shovel and set about filling the tin bucket with coal. What a clatter. I sneezed. My arms ached. My feet were cold, and sore. My jeans were manky. But I've never worked so fast. I remembered everything Noble told me, even though he spoke in practically a foreign accent. With sooty hands I lifted the full bucket and an empty one for the ash then hobbled over the cobbled stones towards the big house.

Noble was right about breaking my back. This was heavier than carrying both the twins together. Heavier than lugging my bike up a hill. I staggered into the house through the back door. It was agony.

My arms had gone numb. But I did it. I reached the first-floor landing and pushed open a door. There was a four-poster bed in the room and a fireplace. I hobbled over to the fireplace, panting like I'd run a marathon. It was full of grey powdery ash. I sunk to my knees and scooped up the ash with an old brush. I coughed and spluttered but kept scooping with ash puffing up and floating everywhere. I got as much as I could and filled the empty bucket. Then I heaped fat pieces of coal onto the fire grate. I struck a match, put it under the coal... and nothing happened. The match flickered then went out. I tried another one. And another.

I felt like crying but suddenly remembered the fire Agnes and I had made for our time travel. It felt like years ago, but this was still the same day. We had used twisted pieces of paper to catch the flame. I looked around frantically for newspapers. I looked under the big bed. Nothing. But next to the bed there was a wooden writing desk. I pulled open the drawers and my eyes fell on a sheet of paper. Suddenly I forgot about newspapers. I should be looking for the deeds! Here I was, *inside* the house. Suddenly finding myself trapped as a servant in 1914 was bad, but looking on the bright side, this was my chance to find out more about this place, and to look for nooks and crannies where title deeds might be hidden away. I know that's how Agnes would see it. From now on, I would be keep my eyes and ears open for any information that might save our den. I'd start with this desk. I opened all the drawers. There were sheets of blank paper in different sizes, envelopes and a leaflet. The leaflet had a grainy black-and-white photo of the house on it, and the words –

TWEEDSIDE HOTEL

A first-class establishment nestled among the sloping and green hills of the Scottish Borders. Magnificent prospects. An ideal retreat for those wishing to get away from the hustle and bustle of life...

Weird. Had the house been a hotel at some stage? Anyway, a leaflet wasn't the deeds. With my heart racing like mad I fumbled about. Was there anything hidden in the desk – false bottoms to the drawers? A concealed drawer anywhere? A locked compartment? No, only the pieces of blank paper. Well, they would do for starting the fire anyway. I twisted some up and stuffed them under the coal. "Please work," I muttered, "please!" With my hand shaking I struck the match and held it under the paper. A small blue flame caught light. I shoved loads more matches into the fire, so they would light and help the coal catch. Thankfully it worked. Gradually one small piece of coal started to glow, but I had used up half the box of matches, and a pile of Gaunt's writing paper.

I grabbed the bucket full of ash, and the bucket that was now half full of coal and hurried on. Next to the bedroom was a kind of living room, with armchairs and a few more stuffed stag heads on the wall. Creepsville! Was there anywhere here that someone might file important papers and then forget about them? I ran my fingers over panelling in case any of it felt loose or sprung open. I lifted a few dusty books then put them back. I slid my fingers under the cushions. There were no important papers.

This fireplace was heaped with ash – more than I could fit in the ash bucket. Noble had said something about spreading it on the compost heap. I grabbed the heavy ash bucket and dashed downstairs.

Outside, I looked around for the compost heap and found it behind the coal shed, up against the high back wall of the garden. It didn't look like a compost heap; it looked like a rubbish tip. Broken chairs and tables lay in a pile, like they were waiting for Guy Fawkes Night. Mingled in with the broken furniture I could see potato peelings, broken plates and raggedy old blankets. I took my bucket of ash and threw it over the rubbish.

I was ready to turn and race back when I heard three whistles from behind the wall. The gang signal. Agnes!

17

I glanced over my shoulder. No one was about. I dropped my ash bucket and ran to the wall beside the rubbishy compost heap. "Agnes?" I hissed, "are you there?"

"Saul! I heard footsteps. Thought I'd try the signal." She was just over on the other side of this great wall.

"Are you ok?"

"Yes, I'm a bit hungry, but I'm ok. What about you?"

I felt like crying. I was not ok. I was sore. I was more than a bit hungry. I was trapped. I was doing work I'd never have imagined doing in my life. "Kinda." I said.

"Meet me at the iron gates at midnight, if you can get out safely. Then we can talk."

Agnes had no idea how difficult that might be. Maybe I would be locked in? But I couldn't stand here talking at the wall. "I'll try," I said.

At that moment a bell clanged. I heard a voice at the back door call out, "Servants' tea time!" I was starving. I grabbed my empty ash bucket and ran.

"So!" In the kitchen, the housekeeper looked me up and down. "We've got a thief for a servant now, have we?"

I didn't know what to say in my own defence. I was too busy re-adjusting my image of Mrs Buchan, who wasn't a six-foot giant after all. She was what you might call stocky, with a broad forehead, tired-looking eyes and a long black dress. She didn't exactly seem pleased to see me.

"Well, come in and have a cup of tea," she said, shaking her head, "and for heaven's sake put down that bucket. I don't want ash all over the kitchen."

Next thing, there I was, in the servant's poky kitchen, drinking tea and wolfing down a biscuit. The homemade shortbread Elsie gave me was probably a few days old. And the tea was stewed, but I was getting used to that. As Mrs Buchan drank her tea she inspected us over the rim of her cup. Then she set her cup down in a saucer. "Gaunt," She announced, "is expecting a foreign guest and has ordered that the whole house be put in perfect order." Elsie sighed. Frank drained his tea. Mrs Buchan shook her head like she didn't approve. "Aye, it is to be warmed up and polished up and for the love of goodness go about your duties smartly and be neither seen nor heard."

"Yes, Mrs Buchan," Elsie mumbled. With that the housekeeper up and left, muttering to herself about how there was so much to be done – and precious few experienced servants to do it, not like the old days when the house had been bursting with housemaids and footmen, scullery maids and groomsmen.

When Mrs Buchan had gone, Elsie got up, fished about in the biscuit tin and next thing placed half a bit of shortbread on my plate, like she was doing me a great favour. If it wasn't for her I would be free to explore 1914 with Agnes, not sit in the servant's kitchen, exhausted. Elsie had been the one yelling and telling on me. Now she was acting like she felt sorry for me.

While I gobbled up the shortbread, Noble leant towards me. "How many more fires you still to lay?"

"Let him finish his biscuit, Frank," Elsie said, "for Lord knows we must have our food. The poor lad is famished."

Frank? Who was Frank? I didn't ask until I'd licked the crumbs and drained the last drop of tea. "Who's Frank?" I said, sitting back.

"Him," said Elsie, pointing at Noble with her fork, "my own dear and good brother. The only family I have in this big wide world."

Noble put his cup down and thrust out his hand across the table. "Frank Noble," he said. "Pleased to meet yea."

"I'm Saul Martin," I said, and shook his hand.

"This here," he nodded to where the little maid sat, "is Elspeth Noble, my dear and good sister."

So I shook her hand too, and for some reason they laughed. Maybe it was my name, or my voice, or the way I shook hands. Maybe they were having me on with this 'dear and good' stuff. Maybe they just thought it was funny that the thief was turning out to be so friendly. Whatever the big joke they laughed so much their shoulders shook. I joined in and soon we had tears rolling down our faces.

Frank was first to stop. Elsie finished with a fit of her coughing.

"Now, Saul Martin," Frank said, all formal, "how many more fires?"

I shrugged. Just thinking about fires and heaving buckets of coal made me tired. My arms seriously ached. It even hurt lifting the cup of tea.

"Ye best get on. Mrs Buchan gave orders. Elsie will be here polishing the spoons. Gaunt is out snooping about down the Mill. Best stoke up the fire in his study. He likes it roaring. Summer, winter, all the same. Tell you what, I'll show you. You've not got much clue, have you, Saul? I watched you working and I says to Elsie, that boy hasn't got a clue."

I wanted to tell him how I was the gang leader. How I could do loads of things. How I could fix bikes and play guitar, take cool photos, shoot films, make pancakes and climb trees. I was good at drawing, and basketball. But I just shrugged and followed him out to the stables. He scooped up a handful of hay. I thought he was going to feed the horses but he stuffed it on top of my coals. "For starting the fire," he said, and sent me on my way.

"Keep at it," Elsie said with a cough as I went back through the kitchen, "or there'll be no porridge for you later."

"Porridge?" I threw her a quizzical frown. Breakfast? It couldn't be morning already – we hadn't slept.

"Aye, porridge, nincompoop," Elsie said, banging the teacups onto the washboard and giggling, "for supper."

Believe it or not, once I got used to the idea, I was actually drooling, looking forward to my evening porridge.

The hay worked. It was just as good as newspaper. Or writing paper. I built up the fire in Gaunt's study and kept going from room to room, carrying buckets, stacking up coal, trying to get the rest of the matches to last. I looked for secret hiding places too. Crevices in alcoves, slots by windows, paintings that didn't hold together properly. I found precisely nothing.

When I was dusting ash on the floor of a parlour room, I found myself thinking about Will and Robbie. I hardly noticed the dust I was pushing about. I thought about going to Paris. How we're actually going to go up the Eiffel Tower and then get a boat along the River Seine. The teacher said we'll also go to the art gallery and see the famous pictures.

Robbie had groaned loudly when the teacher said we were all going to the art gallery. Agnes had said to him afterwards that was pretty ignorant behaviour. They practically got into a fight about it. But they made up the next day. Or rather Agnes made the effort and Robbie came round. She gave him a postcard of the Mona Lisa, which is a famous painting of a woman with a little smile on her face. I mean, it's ok, but I don't quite get why it's worth millions of pounds. Anyway she had written on the back of the postcard:

Dear Robbie, sorry. We are all different. We all like different things. This is a picture of the Mona Lisa. You will see her in the Louvre Art Gallery. Maybe you will like her. So can't wait to go to Paris.

Agnes.

Robbie had muttered thanks and stuffed the postcard into his rucksack. He showed it to me later and I said he should be kind to Agnes. She wasn't well off like he was. I noticed he was definitely friendlier to her after that, and even gave her a bar of chocolate, pretending he didn't want it. Agnes has got a seriously sweet tooth.

The time passed quickly in that gloomy parlour room when I thought about home and how things used to be, though I had swept right round the huge fireplace. I imagined how I could grow rich in 1914 by inventing things like vacuum cleaners. Gaunt House didn't even have electricity. Some houses did, Frank said, but Gaunt House was still in the dark ages. It had gaslights, but Elsie said Gaunt was so mean the lights were never lit from May till September. And when they are, she said, they hiss and stink and hardly give enough light to see your porridge by.

My knees were cold and sore. I went over to the window and looked into the garden. I'd only been in this house one day but it felt like a week. It was so strange to know exactly what it would look like in the future. It wouldn't be long before the weeds would grow, the house would crumble. I glanced up at the wooden beams, imagining them broken, cobwebby and with birds nesting in the rafters.

I heard clanging from the kitchen, like someone was banging two metal lids together. "Porridge!" Elsie shouted.

BANG! BANG! BANG!

I was actually looking forward to it. Maybe it was all this work, but I was ravenous. I would have eaten a horse, or a pigeon. I was so hungry I think I would even have tried frog's legs!

As soon as I had licked that porridge bowl clean I was so ready for bed, but I helped with the cleaning up and watched for a chance to meet Agnes at the gate. Frank had gone out to check the horses had water and Elsie was sitting up in her box bed in the corner of the kitchen doing a cat's cradle with a piece of string. I mumbled a sleepy "Good night!" like I was heading for the damp little cupboard where I was meant to sleep, then I slipped out the back door, into the night.

18

Being midnight, it was really dark in the garden, though I could see a faint light coming through the hut window. The gardener must have a candle burning there in our den. Well, his hut now, but our den in the future. Our den forever, I hoped.

As I hurried up to the tall iron gates I made three low owl calls. I got three calls straight back. Agnes was there waiting, clutching the bars like *she* was the prisoner, not me. It was great to see her. I passed her a crust of bread I'd found in the kitchen.

While she chewed, I poured out everything about Gaunt and Frank and Elsie and coal fires and my tired arms.

"But Saul," she whispered, her voice all muffled, "have you searched for the deeds of the house? Have you, Saul?"

"I've looked in loads of places," I whispered back. "I found a weird thing about this house being a hotel, but I don't think it's the deeds. Agnes," I shot a glance back over my shoulder. "I saw a calendar in the house. The war is going to start in two days. Maybe we should just go. This isn't working out like we thought." Gaunt's 'terms and conditions' were freaking me out, plus I was exhausted. "And," I said. "I don't like being a servant."

"But Saul, think about it, it's perfect." I was ready to go on about how totally not perfect it was, but Agnes was on a roll. "You're actually *in* the house. What an opportunity. Let's try for a bit longer. I'll find out what I can on the outside and you keep looking inside." She had a point. "But for goodness sake, take care," she whispered, uneasily. "The women in the town have been telling me about this place. My gran was right. This house *was* in our family. The horrible man that dragged you off, he cheated my relative. My relative was called John Hogg." Agnes was speaking quite loudly now. Part of me was listening and part of me was listening out for the sound of horse's hooves. "He owned the mill and needed a manager when he got old," she went on. "The women said poor old John went soft in the head. He hired Gaunt to take care of things, and then he got too old and confused to stand up to someone greedy and pushy like Gaunt. They said Gaunt convinced John Hogg that as manager *he* should be living in the big house, and next thing old John Hogg dies and the manager is telling everyone he left the house to him. For the debts of the mill, he said. And the women said many folks are scared of Mr Gaunt and don't want to get in his bad books, because they don't want to lose their jobs at the mill. So he gets away with it. Oh, Saul, imagine if we could find those deeds."

"Ok," I whispered. "I'll stick with it another day. Two at the most. Then let's go back, deeds or no deeds."

"Great! And don't worry about me, Saul. I'm happy in my hiding place. I've got my sleeping bag. And I'm used to adventure." She squeezed my arm. "Goodnight, and keep searching for the deeds, Saul."

I nodded to her through the iron bars though I could hardly see her. She was just a shadowy shape. But I could tell she was waving as she stepped away. "We can do it!" she whispered, and suddenly I felt she was right. We could do it! We were a team: me searching on the inside; her investigating on the outside. I wasn't really a servant. That was just a cover. I was solving a mystery.

Trying not to make a sound, I padded quickly up to the dark house and slipped in the back door. I lay down under my tattered blanket, not bothering to get undressed. In seconds, I was fast asleep.

"Porridge!" Elsie screeched in my ear. It felt like only five minutes had passed since I lay down. I pulled the blanket over my face. "I says 'porridge!'. Get up, deaf muttonhead. It's quarter-past six and you're lying snoring like a lord. Mrs Buchan says rise and shine, you hear?"

Elsie nudged me. She pulled at the blanket, which was so thin it ripped. "Now see what you done. Eejit. It's poor me'll have to put a stitch in that. Idle lie-a-bed. Get up!"

"Leave me alone," I mumbled. I felt like I was stuck to the ground. There was no way my body could get up.

"Up and work or you'll have us all in trouble with the master," said Frank, and they both started tickling me.

"Jeez," I groaned, fighting them off. They were up, dressed and ready for breakfast. Had they even been to sleep?

"You took the Lord's name in vain," Elsie snapped. "You'll be struck down, won't he, Frank?"

But Frank just laughed. "Come on and eat," he called to me, waving a spoon in the air. Ok, I was hungry but couldn't stomach more porridge. It was just bearable the night before. My dad can make good porridge with butter in it, then I pour cream over it and syrup, or if there's no syrup, sugar. Elsie's lumpy porridge is nothing like my dad's.

"For whit we are about tae receive may the Lord mak us truly thankful," Frank droned.

I dragged myself over to the miserable table where their spoons were clattering. They gobbled and made a lot of chewing, licking and slurping sounds. I couldn't get excited about porridge but it was beginning to dawn on me that there was no toast, crispy bacon, croissants, hot chocolate or Cheerios on offer. It was porridge or nothing. So with a scowl on my face I managed a few spoonfuls.

Then Elsie scooped up the bowls and winked at me. "Off to work, laddie. Mrs Buchan's gone to the market in town. She says not to let you near the silver. She says you're to make the fires, and quick!"

I groaned and trudged up the stairs to face another day, and to sweep and lay again all the fires I'd laid yesterday.

Gaunt House had a bit more bustle about it today. Mrs Buchan was insisting that the curtains get a good wash and Elsie was beating the rugs, whacking them with a stick. Frank was sitting on a stone step polishing saddles and boots, whistling to himself. As well as laying the fires I had to polish the fireplaces until they gleamed. I worked hard, but kept reminding myself, I wasn't *really* a servant.

I looked about me as I went from room to room. There were places everywhere that documents could be hidden, but nowhere that seemed likely. I looked behind old picture frames. I slipped my hands down the backs of chairs. I fumbled under beds, but all I found was dust. No deeds and no sign of my mum's ring either.

After making the fires, Mrs Buchan had me peeling potatoes for lunch. I wondered whether chips had been invented yet!

19

Agnes

What a sweet and lovely thing to be woken by a lark singing above me. As well as a pencil sharpener, I had forgotten to pack a watch, but considering I had time travelled a hundred years, a watch would probably be useless. I lay for ages in my warm sleeping bag listening to the singing bird. It wasn't completely light, only half light. The lark sounded like the happiest creature and I forgot today was August 3rd, 1914. I forgot Britain was going to declare war on Germany tomorrow, because they were obliged to, because Germany invaded neutral Belgium, and they'd promised they'd help Belgium, and then so many people would die.

I had slept really well, and felt ready to rise and shine. Plus I got this warm feeling that the lark was singing just for me. A few times he had looked at me, curious probably and pleased for a bit of company. On the other side of the wall I heard a door opening and closing. I scrambled out of my sleeping bag, smoothed down my very crumpled dress and rolled and stuffed the sleeping bag into my rucksack. I then hid the rucksack under the gorse bush. Apart from the pressed-down moss you would never know I had been there. I had this wild hope that Saul was up early and had some breakfast for me – maybe a warm roll and butter, or cake, or orange juice.

I strained my ears like mad and could just make out someone walking on the other side of the wall. It sounded like this person had shoes on – there was a soft tap-tap on the stones – maybe Saul had shoes now. He seemed to be walking round the house. I hurried round the outside of the wall, hid behind a bush and watched the gates. It wasn't Saul, but a woman. My heart sank. She had on a hat and long coat, and carried a basket under her arm. She looked like a smart servant. I peered out from between bits of bush and saw her take out a bunch of keys. She slotted one into the gate lock, opened it with a creak then snapped it shut behind her. She locked it, pocketed the keys and briskly set off, over the open countryside towards town.

I guessed that this was maybe the woman that gossiped with the washerwomen about the house, so I followed her. She didn't even look back.

I paused to have a quick look at the hills of the Borders that I knew so well. They hadn't changed a bit and the day was breaking pale and lovely over the slopes. And there were the spires of the churches and the top of the bridge over the Tweed. For a moment I thought I was back in the twenty-first century.

I hadn't been looking about long, but when I turned

back the woman with the hat and the basket under her arm was gone. From the washerwoman's talk the day before, I guessed she was going to the market.

I knew my way to the High Street. The soles of my bare feet were already hardening and it was getting easier to jump over stones and clumps of grass without it stinging. I clambered over the stone dyke and ran over the field that led to the edge of town. The church bells rang out for six in the morning. I don't think I had ever been out so early, but it seems rising early was common in the past. There were lots of people around. Smoke was already puffing out from the chimneys of the mills. I could hear horses neighing and it sounded like every cockerel in the world had gathered in Peebles for choir practice. All I had to do was follow the noise.

In the High Street there were a good many animals. A man was herding sheep into a wooden makeshift fence and they were **BAA-ING** their woolly heads off. Another man with a long wooden stick was coaxing cows into a stall. They were **MOO-ING** and he was shouting. A group of women with long brown skirts on and scarves around their hair were busy lining up what smelt like barrels of fish. Already some of them were starting to cry out: "Herring, haddock, trout, eels! Come and buy! Come and buy!"

I stroked the silver chain around my neck. I was so hungry I decided to try and sell it to buy food. There was a butcher arranging pigs' heads and pigs' trotters and every bit of pig you could imagine –

except bacon in a vacuum pack from a supermarket. Even the butcher with his pink face looked a bit like a pig. I ventured further along.

Carts pulled by horses were piled high with potatoes and cabbages and leeks and carrots and onions. Everybody was wishing each other a very good morning. There was no sign of the woman from the big house, but my eyes lit up when I saw, sitting among a pile of onions, a girl about my size smile at me. She was plaiting onion stalks and singing:

"Up in the mornings no fir me, up in the morning early..."

"Stop yer complaining," a man shouted. He was arranging his vegetables in pretty shapes on the cart. I guessed he was her father. The girl went on silently stringing up the onions without even glancing up at him.

A woman called out, "Away to the butcher, lassie, and get us a ham shank. A good one mind, none of your scraggy end, tell him." I guessed that was the girl's mother and the girl seemed happy enough to lay down her onions and hop down from the cart. She skipped along the High Street, in no hurry to get that ham shank. I followed her, and skipped too. Soon we were skipping side by side.

"We'll get a game of peevers soon," she said, like she had known me for ages. "I got good stones for skiting." She patted the pocket of her apron. I smiled and skipped some more. "Then," she went on, waving to the men at the baker's stall, "we can go down the river and play chuckie stanes."

I worked that one out. Chucking stones. I smiled. "Guid," I said, trying to sound like her, "that would be just grand." The smell of fresh bread was making me feel light-headed. I unclipped the tiny silver chain from around my neck. It had belonged to my mother, but I knew she wouldn't want me to go hungry. I swung it in front of the girl. "Where's the best place to sell this?"

The girl froze and stared at the silver chain. "You pinched that, did yea?"

I shook my head and clasped it to me, and just to prove the point tears welled up in my eyes. "It was my own dead mother's," I said with a little sob. I wasn't acting. I really did feel sad.

Next thing the girl wrapped her arm around my shoulder. "You poor lassie," she said. "My own mother clips me about the ear for next to nothing, but if she died I would die too, of a broken heart." I thought she was going to burst into tears.

"But I have an auntie," I said quickly, "Jean Burns."

"Yea mean that herb-wifie down at Walkershaugh?"

I nodded and the girl hugged me even tighter. "My mither says she could raise the dead with all her salves and ointments." Then she whispered in my ear, "Donald Christie. Along next to the fishmonger. He's always after a bit o' silver. He'll give you a pretty penny for it. Tell him Peggy Bell sent you, then he won't cheat you."

"Thank yea," I said, and slipped away. I turned to

wave then hurried along the High Street, darting in and out between stalls and smells and feeling so hungry I thought I might faint. I planned on buying buns with strawberry jam smeared on top. Loads and loads of buns.

It was easy to follow my nose and find the fishmongers. Phew! What a stink. Fish shops in the future never smelt so strong. I pulled myself away from the fish and worked out that the man at the next stall was Donald Christie. He had white hair and a beard, and was sitting on a wooden box and smoking a pipe. At first glance it was hard to tell what kind of stall his was. He'd laid out brooches and hatpins and china dogs and candlesticks. The smoke from his pipe was pretty strong and wafted right into my face. I couldn't believe how smelly the past was, or was it me being so hungry that made everything so overwhelming? "Morning," he said and sucked loudly on his pipe.

"Morning," I replied.

"It'll stay fine till noon, then I daresay it'll break. Then we'll have a shower. Or two."

I looked up at the sky, wondering whether he could forecast the war as well as showers. "Aye," I said, "I think you're right."

"Not seen you afore," he said, eyeing me inquisitively. "Not from these parts, eh?"

"Staying with my aunt for the summer," I blurted out, feeling my palms sweat. "I have a silver necklace." I held it out over the stall. "How much would you give me for it?"

His eyes lit up. "Have to have a good old peek at it first, won't I?" I dropped it into his outstretched palm. He brought a huge magnifying glass up to his eye and peered closely at my necklace. "Not bad," he said, still sucking on his pipe. "Not bad craftsmanship." He peered from me to the necklace.

"It was my mother's," I explained, "and hardship has forced me to sell it."

He hummed and hawed. "Sixpence ha'penny," he said, "not a farthing less and that's good clean money too."

I had studied currency, and sixpence ha'penny was hardly a fortune, even in 1914. I knew my necklace was worth more than that. Suddenly the man gasped and brought the bracelet even closer to his huge magnifying glass. "There's been some hallmarking error," he said, "it is marked 1979."

"1879," I said, too hastily. "I mean, that's what it should say. Easy to mix up an eight and a nine, eh?" I smiled at him and swiftly went on. "Peggy Bell said you would give me a lot more than sixpence ha'penny."

He looked flustered for a moment then nodded. "Mistakes all round this merry morning. Here's the date wrong, and here's me meaning to say one shilling and sixpence. What was I thinking? It's August madness, that's what it is."

"August madness right enough," I said and skipped away from Donald Christie's bric-a-brac stall with one shilling and sixpence in my hand. In modern money that is only about thirteen pence, but in 1914 it could buy a lot.

I bought fresh buns. Sitting down by the mercat cross I stuffed a warm one into my mouth. I didn't care that I looked famished. I was famished. I chewed and swallowed and with every bite felt better and better. With my cheeks stuffed like a squirrel's I saw the woman I had been following from the big house. She was bustling past with parcels under her arm and bread in the basket. That bit of food I'd had gave me courage so, swallowing fast, I ran over to her. "Hello," I blurted out. "Thought I saw you come from the big house over the field." The woman frowned at me and puckered her lips. She looked ready to stride off, so quickly I said, "And I wondered if you need a scullery maid? I'm a good worker, and honest." She looked me up and down. "I can wash dishes and pots, and dry them too. I'm very careful," I went on, smiling, and making myself as tall as I could.

"Might do," she said, or snapped more like, but that didn't put me off. I kept smiling, kept thinking of being with Saul and finding the deeds.

"I can also scrub and sweep, cook and launder," I said, "I'm not afraid of hard work. Not one bit."

She frowned, stared at me again, then nodded. "Call round at the house tomorrow. Say Mrs Buchan sent for you." With that she marched off and vanished into the crowd. An even bigger smile spread over my face. If I wasn't mistaken, I, thirteen-year-old Agnes Brown, had a job!

20

Agnes

I sunk my teeth into another bun. I still had six left, and planned on saving some till tomorrow and sharing them with Saul and the other poor servants.

Feeling pretty chuffed, I ambled towards the river. I looked to see if the girl called Peggy Bell was chucking stones into the river. She was and waved, but when she beckoned for me to come over I shook my head. I had things to do. Like finding a great-great-great-great aunt, for instance.

Peggy Bell had said Jean lived in Walkershaugh. That's a road, and it was easy enough to find, but I had no idea what number house to knock at. I wandered along past the stone cottages, gazing at the pretty little violets and pansies in the gardens. A woman in a flowery-patterned pinny was outside one house, polishing her brass doorbell.

"Lovely morning," I piped up.

The woman swung round and peered at me. "For now," she said, curtly, and breathed on the brass.

"Can you tell me where, um, Jean lives?" I blurted out. "Please?"

The woman eyed me again. "What do you want with Jean? If that's a parcel for her you can leave it here."

I didn't know what to say. I shook my head and held on tightly to the brown paper bag of rolls. "No. It's not, um, a parcel. I just wanted… to bring her greetings from a distant relative."

The woman stopped polishing. "Oh, aye, and where would that be from, then?"

I flung an arm vaguely to the north. "Edinburgh," I said.

"Oh, Edinburgh? I didn't know the auld wifie had kin in Edinburgh. Anyway, Jean's no in." I saw the woman nod to the small stone cottage opposite. "I'll tell her yea came looking fir her. What's yer name?"

"Mind your own business. Jeannie's here." I swung round and stared at a woman who was standing behind me on the street. I hadn't heard her approach. She had thick grey hair that tumbled, kind of wild looking, all the way past her shoulders, and she wore a long green dress. She looked like she had stepped out of the forest. I could see bits of moss sticking to her dress and her hair. She had a twinkle in her eye and she smiled at me. It was the same woman I had seen when I had been singing on the street. "It's alright Mrs Gilchrist," she called out, "I'm home," then she linked her arm in mine and, like a long-lost chum, led me over the road and into her little garden. "Nosy old bat," she said, taking me into the house. "Everybody else's business is always more interesting than her own. Here, have a seat on that old chair, lassie, and tell me what I can do for you."

It felt cosy inside. The place smelt of geraniums, and all kinds of other flowers. Jean made herself comfy in an old chair and now she was gazing at me, smiling, and waiting for my story. Somehow, looking at my great-great-great-great aunt and her being so soft and her eyes so kind, I couldn't spin any lie like I'd planned to. If anybody on this planet was not going to bat an eyelid about time travel, I had the feeling it was her. "Did you ever hear of Agatha Black?" I began.

"Indeed I did. Many in Peebles held her in high esteem. Such a kind person, and a bonny mother by all accounts. Some say she took a journey into the future. Sometimes I sit here, brewing my healing herbs, and wonder if she might appear." Jean laughed gently. "You have heard the stories too?"

I took a deep breath, then out it came, rushing and tumbling, but Jean listened to every word. "Agatha came to me. And now, I have come to you. I live in the future. I live in a caravan and go to school, and I'm quite good at school, and I'm in a gang and I have friends now. We have a den and Saul is the gang leader. He's here too – in the past I mean. We can travel through time. My name is Agnes Brown. My dad is Michael. His mother is my gran, Jessica. Her mother was called Joanna. Joanna's mother was called Grace. Grace's poor mother, Eliza, died in childbirth. Eliza was married to John Hogg."

I stopped talking and gazed at this kind woman who was nodding her head and patting me on the back of my hand. "I know," she murmured, "for precious Eliza was my sister." She fell silent so I waited, then gently pressed her hand.

"So, you are my great-great-great-great aunt?"

Jean nodded. "Indeed I am, child. When Grace was born with no mother to care for her," she said quietly, "I helped Mr Hogg in Yew Tree House. He could never have coped."

"Where's Yew Tree House?" I asked.

Jean smiled. "The very place Gaunt has claimed for his own."

My heart skipped a beat.

Jean saw that I was flustered. "Aye," she went on, smiling warmly at me, "John Hogg loved that tree. 'Twas him named the house after it. He told me he spent his childhood playing around it. In his old age he would often wander down to the yew tree. Sometimes he talked to it!"

"We like it too," I said.

"That yew has stood on that spot for hundreds of years. It knows about time." Jean nodded, as if she knew about time too, and her green eyes sparkled.

"But, what happened to Grace?"

"Well, old John had enough, what with the mill to run and what do men know of bringing up children?" She smiled but I could see the pain flit across her eyes. "So it was myself and Margaret

Buchan, the housekeeper, who brought up that darling child. She was a bonnie wee thing." Jean looked into the distance, like she was seeing the girl again. "She played about the yew tree too. Anyway, when Grace was eighteen she fell in love and married. Her husband said they were to travel over the sea to start a new life in Canada. Many went then. Well, Grace begged me to go with them. I was sorely torn. I could see John Hogg was not well. I could see the mill was badly run, but what could a woman do? And Mr Hogg assured me he would manage. He was about to employ a manager. The manager would ensure everything was running smoothly. 'Go, Jeanie,' old John Hogg said to me, 'for I wouldn't rest in my grave if you didn't help my dearest daughter.' So I took a ship to Canada. I became nursemaid and housekeeper for my dear niece. I helped nurse her little babe." She pressed my hand again and nodded. "Yes, you are right. Joanna is the little one's name. But when word reached us that John Hogg was poorly, I took a ship back. Grace of course sorely wished to, but what could she do? She had a small baby, and her husband a good job in Toronto. So they stayed and I returned to Scotland. But the ship took six weeks to cross the sea and I was too late. When I arrived back, my brother-in-law John Hogg was already dead, and the house was in the hands of his new manager..." Jean's face darkened, "a Mr Gaunt." She shook her head. "Poor Mrs Buchan was distraught."

"It's kind of our house too. Well, not our house,

but our gang hut is the gardener's hut, near the house. That's our den. And we play in the garden. We play by the yew tree too. But in the future, developers are planning on building luxury flats in the garden, because they say nobody actually owns the land. But…"

"But, under this law that gives property only to male heirs," Jean said, now smiling at me, "your father should, by rights, inherit the house and the land."

I nodded, my heart beating fast. "It's a ruin now. I mean, in a hundred years it is a terrible ruin. But we like it like that. And the garden is a wilderness. It's our jungle. We climb the trees and we have a rope swing. Our den leans a bit to the side, but it's cosy. It's great fun. We have to find the deeds to the house. That's why we came back to 1914."

Jean gazed into the distance, twisting a long curl of hair around her finger. "You took a great risk."

"But we had to do something. Even if we never find the deeds, at least we tried."

"You are a brave lass. Better to take a risk than live with regrets." Then she smiled at me and said, "A cup of tea, Agnes?"

Which seemed like a brilliant idea. But then I remembered the date, and it seemed wrong to relax in a comfy armchair, sipping tea. "There's going to be a war," I blurted out, "a really terrible war."

Jean nodded sadly. "I know."

21

Later that morning, Mrs Buchan, back from the market, rang a bell. We rushed down and had to line up by the back door. The housekeeper eyed us sternly. Especially me. "Elsie, get the needle and thread out and put a few stitches in that old suit of your brother's. We can't have Blackie looking a disgrace."

I could feel my cheeks turning beetroot under the grime and soot. She was right. I was a mess. My jeans were black. My good T-shirt was all torn and stained.

"Yes, Mrs Buchan," Elsie chanted.

"We all need to smarten up around here. For apparently," she said, with a sigh, "this place is a hotel now. I told you about the foreign guest. Well, I'm told, he will be arriving in a few days – and has requested peace and quiet." She seemed pretty tight-lipped and disapproving about it all. "There's to be no sleeping on the job." She eyed Frank. "And no coughing and spluttering in public." She turned her beady eye on Elsie. "On no account must you disturb the guest. And remember, be neither seen nor heard. Now," she clapped her hands, "off to work." Then she marched off, leaving us to hurry back to the kitchen.

"It's happened," said Elsie, lowering herself onto

the bench. "Gaunt was always going on and on about making this place a hotel. We thought it wis a joke, didn't we, Frank? We thought he was pie-in-the-sky about guests. But, oh Lord above, one's coming." She looked ready to burst into tears and had a coughing fit instead. "That'll be the last straw for Mrs Buchan. She'll leave, and we'll have to do even more work."

Frank patted her on the back and gave her a hug. Poor Elsie. She was probably suffering from malnutrition. Her legs were like pins. You could see the bones in her face. Maybe she was older than ten? Suddenly I remembered that leaflet I had seen about magnificent views and peace and quiet. "Tweedside Hotel," I mumbled.

"Whit you on about?" Frank stared at me. So did Elsie.

"This place," I said. "I saw a leaflet. Gaunt is calling this house 'Tweedside Hotel.'"

Frank snorted at that and Elsie frowned. "Whit's a – a leaflet?" she asked.

I was getting ready to explain about leaflets and brochures and stuff when Mrs Buchan came bustling into the kitchen. She had Frank's old suit in her arms and set it down on the table in front of Elsie. "Patch up the elbows," she ordered then turned and glared at me. "We'll need you decent for when the guest arrives. Meanwhile, Blackie, set fires in the rooms on the second floor. That's where the important guest is to be put up."

So, after throwing more coals onto the master's fire, I went upstairs. There was bustle up and down the second-floor hallway with Mrs Buchan busy changing the bed and airing out rooms. She barked at me to start clearing the fireplace and sweep the floor in the room at the far end.

I heard her mutter as I hurried along the hallway. "The sooner you're in a proper suit of clothes, the better." I wasn't so sure about that. My own clothes were covered in soot, but at least they were mine.

All thoughts of clothes vanished as soon as I entered that big room. Heavy velvet curtains were drawn, leaving a gap in the middle where a finger of light keeked through and stroked the dusty floor. The room seemed pretty bare, just a couple of lounge-around sofas and a chair. It was only when I opened the curtains I saw that the room wasn't completely empty. In the corner was a huge wooden chest. The deeds! I fell to my knees and fumbled with the metal catch, my heart thumping. This was the ideal place to store important documents. I listened out for the housekeeper and shook my bucket of coal, making out like I was hard at work. The chest opened with a creak and I was gaping down at piles of yellowing paper. I was right! This had to be deeds!

I picked up one sheet of paper, then another. Then another. My hopes sank. It looked like I had discovered somebody's art box. The chest was full of old drawings. Plants and gardens, as far as I could make out, and not very talented either. I kept rummaging through the musty-smelling old papers: flowers, trees and more trees. Then I saw one I knew – it was a drawing of the yew tree – our yew tree! And it was pretty good.

It looked like the artist had spent ages on it, shading thick drooping branches and intricate roots. This masterpiece was even signed – *John Hogg* Wow! And at the edge of the paper I could just make out faded writing – *strong protection*. Weird! There were more words, but I couldn't read them. I had the drawing right up to my face, trying to, when suddenly I heard a cough behind me.

22

"Once a thief," I dropped the paper and swung round, "always a thief." Mrs Buchan was towering over me. My mind raced.

"Um… I'm trying to… find old paper to start the fire." She wasn't impressed. Next thing she bent down and slammed the chest shut. I pulled my fingers away just in time.

"Not *that* paper," she snapped. "Open that chest once more and I'll report you to the master. Do you understand?"

"Yes, Mrs Buchan," I mumbled. She shot me a final glare then turned and stomped out. With Gaunt's terms and conditions sharp in my mind, I hurried over to set the fire.

When I got back downstairs, Elsie was gazing up at her brother. She looked even paler than usual. "I don't trust water from the standpipe, you know that Frank." He was standing over her with a glass in his hands.

"I've heard water is a tonic," Frank said, shoving it in front of her face. "Now swig it down and huld yer nose if you don't like the taste."

Elsie was eyeing it suspiciously and screwing up her face. "Suppose it's got a fly in it."

Frank peered into it. "No fly," he reported. "No muck, no sand, no blinking frog. Nothing but water, as clear as the pebbles whit fall from dark clouds." Then he grinned at her but I could tell it was a put-on grin.

Elsie took the glass and held it at arm's length, like the liquid might suddenly erupt. "Now, that would be a fine thing, wouldn't it, Frank?"

"Whit?"

"To get three wishes from this water. First I'd change this into wine, like whit Jesus did."

Frank laughed at that.

"Then, I'd wish for you to find yourself a better position, Frank. In a fine big stable with plenty grub." She gazed into the water and swirled it. "Then… well, then I'd wish…" She gazed up at her brother and smiled. "I'd wish to be a lady and spend all day strolling in the park then sitting with my feet up after dinner and embroidering handkerchiefs."

"For the love of God, Elsie, just drink the stuff, will you. Else our dinner's cold."

And she did, she drained every last hopeful drop of it, and maybe the water really was a tonic because she suddenly jumped to her feet. "Dinner is served," she announced, though the truth was dinnertime was a dreary affair. Frank used that word and I liked it: 'dreary'.

Elsie spooned out a few grey, sad-looking potatoes and a dollop of over-boiled stinking cabbage. I saw her cut a small piece of grey meat in half. She kept eyeing me sideways to make sure I couldn't see what she was up to. She shuffled across to her brother and dropped a tiny scrap of meat onto his plate where he quickly hid it under the cabbage. I could see it all.

"Keep your scabby meat," I said.

Elsie looked a bit ashamed at that, and quickly muttered the prayer. "Fir whit we are aboot tae receive may the Lord mak us truly thankful."

"Amen," said Frank. They both eyed me.

"Amen," I muttered, then stared down at the food glumly.

Was I, Saul Martin, the fussy eater who liked scampi and chips, meat-feast pizza, chicken tikka masala, Tunnocks Tea Cakes, Irn Bru, pancakes and maple syrup, really going to tuck in to stinking cabbage and grey potatoes? Porridge was bad enough. But I could wish all I liked. Scampi and chips was not on the menu and I had been working for hours. I was starving.

"Waste not, want not," said Frank, stretching his hand toward my plate.

That did it. I grabbed the fork and stabbed a potato. He pulled his hand back just in time. Then I shovelled it into my mouth and it didn't taste too terrible.

When that dismal dinner was done, Frank got up and went to the door. He opened it an inch and looked out, like a soldier on sentry duty. "Mrs Buchan is in her room. Gaunt's horse is out the stable. His majesty's down the Cross Keys for a pint of ale, I'll wager," he told us. Then he winked at me, fished a key out of his pocket and slipped out into the corridor.

"We deserve a good pudding," Elsie whispered, then giggled as she stacked up the plates, but the giggling brought on a little fit of coughing. So I cleared up the plates and let her sit down.

Good puddings I have loved flashed through my mind. Knickerbocker glories came top. Then banoffee pie and cream, then key lime pie with chocolate ice cream, then sticky toffee pudding with vanilla cream custard.

"Ta-da! Spotted Dick, no less!" Frank announced, as he slunk back into the kitchen and handed us each a slice of what looked like mouldy sponge with raisins in it.

"My favourite!" cheered Elsie and sunk her teeth in with relish.

I had given up being fussy and did the same. The three of us sat there in silence, apart from the fairly loud chewing and swallowing sounds.

Frank Noble was first to finish. He patted his pocket and grinned at me. "Got a slice for your wee sister, right here."

So he knew about Agnes? Of course he knew. She had tended to his knee back when I first ran into him. And maybe Elsie had spied her in the town, when I got arrested, and told her brother.

But suddenly I pictured my real wee twin sisters, Ellie and Esmé, and felt this sudden pang of homesickness. I knew I couldn't stay long in the past. Already, in this short time, my real home was fading and this strange life with Frank Noble and his sister Elsie seemed more real than Mum and Dad and the twins and the den and school. I had forgotten exactly what Will and Robbie looked like.

"A penny for them," said Frank.

I shook my head.

"Your thoughts," he said. "Yea were miles away."

I snapped out of it.

"How long's the master away fir, Frank?" I asked him. It was an effort trying to speak old fashioned.

Frank shrugged. "Who knows?"

I got up. "Can I take the..." I racked my brains trying to remember what it was called, "...spotty sick to... to my sister?"

They both burst out laughing again. "He's soft in the heid," said Elsie, looking like she was going to fall off her chair. "Spotty sick!" And they both roared. Frank was chucking his cap up in the air and catching it. Elsie was hugging her sides like they ached.

"Where's she hiding, anyway?" Frank said, suddenly serious. Elsie stopped laughing too, and they both stared at me. "Your sister was with you. I saw her." At that, Frank patted his knee, like he was tenderly remembering Agnes's little nursing deed.

"She's behind the wall," I said. I wanted to tell them the truth. After sharing stolen pudding and having a laugh, it felt like we were friends. "She's... um... not actually my sister. I mean... we're friends, her and me. We're in a gang... we..." They stared up at me, their thin faces half in shadow and half lit with an orange glow from the candle. I glanced over to the window, then over my shoulder to the kitchen door. All was still in Gaunt House. Mrs Buchan was in her room up in the attic, probably writing long letters applying for new jobs, according to Frank. "Actually," I said, "we're from the future."

"I reckoned there was something odd about you," Frank said, but I saw how he moved back a bit, like he didn't trust me.

"Didn't I say he was soft in the heid?" Elsie laughed again, and coughed, and Frank reached over and patted her on the back. "Maybe – it was the… the asylum you ran away from, not… the Poor House. Was it?" she said through her little splutterings.

Maybe half the truth would be easier to swallow? "What I meant to say was, we're from the… the Footer. Footer Hills." I waved my hand like these mythic hills were miles away. "And we found out stuff about Mr Gaunt, and we need to find the deeds of this house. You know, the papers that say who really owns it. Because Mr Gaunt doesn't. Not really. He's a cheat. And you shouldn't be treated like this. Working so hard and eating porridge and cabbage. It's not right. What kind of life is this?" I was on a roll now. "And you," I said, thrusting my hand out towards Elsie, "should be in hospital. *And* you should go to school. Not work for nasty cheating Mr Gaunt."

"I went to school," Elsie said, thrusting out her chin proudly. "Course I did. I can do my letters, and numbers. And I can do a bit of stitching too." Her eyes shot to the drab-looking patched-up suit laid over a chair waiting for me. "Aye," she went on, "I went to school till I was nearly fourteen. I know all about Napoleon, and Mary Queen of Scots. Test me!" Could she seriously be fourteen? Older than me and Agnes! She only looked about ten, but I bet she did know about Mary Queen of Scots, more than me anyway. "She was a Catholic whit got her head chopped off." Elsie was looking pretty pleased with herself. "I'm fourteen and a half, or thereabouts. Isn't that right, Frank?"

Frank nodded. "We know our place," he said but I could see from the way he punched his fist into his hand he felt angry. He knew as well as anyone that Gaunt was a nasty piece of work. "And we've no money for doctors. And Gaunt says he's no money for doctors neither. So Elsie here's got me to watch over her. I do half her chores." Elsie nodded appreciatively at that and patted his arm, then they both fixed their eyes on me. "But now you're here, frae… Footer," Frank raised his eyebrows at that, "you can muck in." Elsie gave her brother an adoring look then reached over and hugged him.

While they hugged, I picked up the jacket Elsie had fixed for me and pulled it on, then the baggy trousers. I looked down at myself, patched up like a scarecrow. As I gazed down at this different Saul I got this horrible feeling, now that I was beginning to seriously look the part, that I might be here for the rest of my life, and I would probably forget that I had ever had another existence. It would fade like a dream. I'd be a nobody, lost in time.

Frank looked up and saw me in my 1914 clothes, but before he could make any comment I dropped the next bombshell. "We heard news of something else. Something that's going to change everything."

"What's that?" Frank said, a protective hand on his sister's shoulder.

"There's going to be a war."

"You think I don't know that?" Frank pushed himself

to his full height, which was about the same height as me though he seemed a bit older than all of us. "The folk in the town talk of little else. But we're going to sort out them Huns, no question!" And with that he ran round the table, whipped up a knife and slashed it through the air like he was sword-fighting a ghost.

Elsie clapped her hands and cheered. "Slay the Hun!" she cried and punched her little fist in the air. "Chop off their heads, Frank. Let them know who's boss round here."

Then Frank wiped the blade of the kitchen knife across his trousers, bowed low, got more sisterly applause, and put the knife back on the sideboard.

"You deserve a medal from the King," Elsie said. "Doesn't he?" She beamed round at me. "With brave men like Frank Noble, Scotland is in safe hands." Elsie, in a party mood, sang a wheezing verse of:

"Rule Brittania!
Brittania rules the waves!
Britons never never ne-ver shall be slaves!"

With Frank doing a wee jig about the kitchen.
"Join in!" Elsie shouted, but I didn't know the words.

2₃

Agnes

A mobile phone would come in really handy. Saul sounds a bit frightened whenever we speak, and from what the women down at the green told me, he's got reason to be. Mr Gaunt runs the mill and he sure gets his money's worth out of the poor workers. Seems like he puts fear into everyone. Wouldn't it be a treat to meet a rich person who was actually kind? Anyway, I am more and more convinced that Gran was right: John Hogg owned the house! But because he was unwell and confused, seems like it was easy enough for a sneak like Gaunt to sway him and tell him how to run his business. The women told me that when Mr Hogg was dying, Mr Gaunt kept trying to get his hands on the deeds of the house. Seems like Gaunt was doing anything to wheedle the whereabouts of the deeds out of Mr Hogg, but the last laugh of it all is that Mr Hogg – bless him – was losing his memory and forgot where he had hid the deeds. All he knew was that they were stored away somewhere safe! Somewhere special, that's all he could remember! It seems nobody knows actually where the deeds are – so Mrs Buchan told the washerwomen. They have a gossip on market days, when she comes in to town to buy provisions (this means food). I saw her there today. Gaunt says the house is his, and Mr Hogg left no male heir so there is no one to contest him, the washerwomen told me. Well, I just smiled at the women, thinking to myself – actually, there IS one male heir. Because I have done my homework. Back in 2014, I went to Peebles museum and searched my family tree. Mr John Hogg has one male heir – Michael Brown, my dad.

Dear diary,

I wish Saul would turn up. I know I did say to him that I was happy in my hiding place. That wasn't a complete lie, my sleeping bag is cosy and the grass under me is soft. Earlier I was happy, and excited, but right now I can't sleep for thinking about the war. Plus there is an owl in a tree nearby that keeps hooting. At first I thought it was Saul, but it isn't. It's a real owl and it feels like an omen — an ill omen. Then there is the poem that Mrs Johnston told us. It's going round and round in my head. And in the poem it isn't an owl that is hooting, it's gas shells, and it's terrible. I read about what gas can do to people and it burns your skin and eats your flesh. And when the poet writes about old beggars under sacks, knock-kneed and coughing like hags, he's writing about boys who are maybe nineteen.

Or twenty. They are so young, but they are limping and blind — like they suddenly grew very old. And here I am, snug in my sleeping bag and boys who tonight are cosy in their beds will soon be in the trenches. Will said how there was no way he would go to war, but Will isn't here. Life is different in 1914. More different than I imagined. When I get back I'll tell him that. I'll tell him how young folk are keen to do their duty and how men whistle tunes in the street.

I tried to remember a happy tune to blot out the poem, but it kept coming back. For ages I lay there, behind the garden wall, till I had remembered all the lines Mrs Johnston had recited to us. I tried to remember what Mrs Johnston looked like but her face kept fading. All I could hear was her voice: "This is the beginning of a famous poem. It was written by Wilfred Owen, a poet and a soldier of the First World War.

Bent double, like old beggars under sacks,
Knock-kneed, coughing like hags, we cursed through sludge,
Till on the haunting flares we turned our backs,
And towards our distant rest began to trudge.
Men marched asleep. Many had lost their boots,
But limped on, blood-shod. All went lame; all blind;
Drunk with fatigue; deaf even to the hoots
Of gas-shells dropping softly behind."

I felt so sad thinking how, because a few people are power-hungry, millions of young people 'doing their duty' are going to die. And not just people, horses too! And it's all going to begin tomorrow.

Eventually the owl stopped hooting.

Then suddenly I heard three whistles, and this wasn't a bird. It was Saul. I was sure of it. I switched my torch off and stuffed my diary and precious pencil down inside my sleeping bag.

I whistled in reply and scrambled up.

"Agnes," Saul whispered loudly, "I brought you some pudding."

Great. I was starving, but I imagined the pudding would break up if he lobbed it over the wall. I couldn't bear to lose it. "Meet me round at the gate," I whispered back, "then you can pass it through. And Saul, I need to tell you about John Hogg and about the market." By now the moon was up and it was possible to see a tiny bit. There were also a zillion stars.

"Ok," Saul murmured. "But if you hear a horse, hide. Gaunt's gone out. He could come back any time."

"Race you to the gates," I said, and suddenly, running near the den like that, it felt like we were back in our normal time. I got to the gates first. There I was, holding the bars like a prisoner and peering through eagerly waiting for him and pudding. I heard him before I saw him, footsteps padding on the stones. Then I spied a shadowy figure. "Saul!" I cried out, feeling so happy to see him. It was pretty dark but I could tell right away that Saul had an old-fashioned suit on. He looked like a proper servant now and I couldn't help giggling.

"Sssh." He glanced over his shoulder. He looked jittery. "Just don't mention the clothes, Agnes, ok?" he whispered, shoving the crumbly cake through the bars of the gate. Like a starving beggar I took it and sunk my teeth into it.

"Ok," I promised. "But listen, Saul, my gran was right." My mouth was full of cake. "That Gaunt man pretends he owns this house. But Hogg put the deeds away somewhere really safe, then couldn't remember where. Somewhere special, that's all he said. Can you believe it, Saul? And Saul, I've met my great-great-great-great aunt; I've got to tell you all about her." I knew I was gabbling on and doubted whether I was making much sense. Plus I was talking with my mouth full. "Saul, did you know—"

Hooves.

We froze and stared at each other through the iron bars.

"He's coming," Saul whispered. "That's Gaunt! He mustn't see us out here. He'll…"

"That's two horses," I whispered, "listen." We both stood, our ears pricked up in the night wind. Eight hooves rumbled and pounded toward us.

"Hide!" Saul hissed.

24

I hid behind a bush. I shoved into it and tried not to yell out as the prickles scratched my hands and ankles. I heard Agnes scarper. The drumming noise of horses' hooves came closer and closer.

"I expected you in a day or two," I heard Gaunt say. "Forgive me, I had not understood when, in your letter, you said 'soon', it would be *this* soon. The rooms may not be quite ready. But you will have complete privacy, and this is indeed a pleasant town for country walks and taking the air."

"I prefer to see hereabouts by bicycle," I heard an American voice say. "You have one. In the advertisement for this hotel you did say 'Guests are welcome to make use of the bicycle.'"

"Certainly," Gaunt replied, as the horses drew to a halt by the gates. I picked up anxiety in his voice.

I've never seen a bicycle here. And because I've been searching for the deeds, I've been into pretty much all the rooms and the sheds.

The horses whinnied and pounded the ground.

"Anything you need, Mr Inglis, just ask."

"And you have installed the telephone? They are all the rage in America."

"I am, ah, thinking of installing one, certainly," Gaunt bluffed, "but I believe these, ah, telephones will be more trouble than they are worth. If we wish to communicate we have letters, have we not? And you will find, should you wish to post a letter, that we have here in Scotland a most excellent postal service. Rest assured sir, you will have everything you need at Tweedside Hotel."

Then I heard Gaunt jump to the ground, his feet landing with a soft thud. I heard a jangle of keys and the creaking sound of the huge iron gates being opened. At least Agnes would be safe once they came through. She could slip away then.

"Peace and quiet, Mr Gaunt, sir, is what I need." The guest said 'Gont' rather than 'Gaunt', but I got a weird feeling about his accent. It was a heavy American one and then in patches it wasn't at all. I've spent enough hours glued to American TV and films (my dad and I watch The Simpsons together – I've seen almost all of them *and* I saw the Lego movie just last weekend) to know a phoney voice when I hear one.

"Let us take a night cap in the drawing room," I heard Gaunt say. There was a slight panic under his words. The guest's rooms were definitely not ready. I bet there was no such thing as a bicycle, and I knew there was no fire alight up there right now. It had taken me ages to do the fires in Gaunt's rooms again this evening, plus I had been helping Elsie. I needed to get back into the coal shed quick, fill up a pail of coal and be seen working.

As the two men on horseback passed the bush where I was hiding and carried on towards the house,

I listened for Agnes. Sure enough I heard the three whistles, very quiet. I whistled back. She replied with two calls, which was a kind of over-and-out. I guessed she was going back to her sleeping bag. I pictured it snug and safe. It wasn't a cold night, and it wasn't raining. I did an owl **HOOT** – the gang call for goodnight.

Then I made a run for it. As they were busy round at the stables, I nipped in the front door. The place looked like it was expecting company. The gaslamps were hissing out a flickering greenish light. There was even a vase of flowers on a small table at the foot of the stairs. I ran down the corridor towards the kitchen. I was learning fast about servants and masters and knew Gaunt would bring his important guest to the front door. Back doors were for the likes of us. Probably Frank, muttering "Yes sir, no sir," would be bent double under luggage. And probably Mrs Buchan would open the front door with a bow and welcome the American. Probably the gardener had tidied the flowerbeds. And probably Elsie was spitting on the silver spoons to polish them. So probably Saul Martin had better get a move on with the fires.

I legged it to the coal shed. No such thing as a gaslight here. But my eyes were getting used to seeing in the dark. The moon threw ghostly shadows about the shed. I fired a few lumps of coal into a bucket then grabbed it. I could hear the horses whinny and I could hear Frank's voice. The stables were close by. It sounded like he was brushing down the horses. I nipped over. "Hey, Frank, how's it going?" I asked, forgetting to speak old fashioned.

But Frank didn't seem to notice. "They're here," he

said, his face up close to the big dark face of a horse. "I never met an American afore," he spoke more to the horse than me, "and dinna mind if I never meet one again. So much for an important gentleman. Ha! He didna say 'Good evening'. There wis me holding his horse and helping him down. Not so much as a farthing tip for me, lifting his bulky bag down. He practically snatched it back off me, like I was some kind of common thief." Frank shot me a glance. "Sorry," he muttered, like I might take offence. "Then Gaunt bustles over and says how Mr Inglis is perfectly happy to carry for himself, then Gaunt hisses in my ear: 'Be neither seen nor heard, Noble.' Blooming cheek. The way he went on about the blinking American I thought I was going to be rich. I thought he'd be tipping us all pounds."

"Yeah, blooming cheek," I said. "Anyway, I better do the fires, eh?"

"I'll give you a hand," said Frank. "Goodnight Midnight," he muttered, patting the big black horse. Then he reached over and patted the other one. "Goodnight Trickster. Sweet dreams."

We hurried over the cobbled yard towards the house. I heard the horses neigh, like they were saying goodnight back to Frank, and I had this horrible image of all the thousands of horses that would soon be dying, caught in the crossfire in the First World War.

"The gents are taking a dram of whisky in the drawing room," Frank whispered as we padded along the back corridor, slinking into the shadows when we passed the drawing room. Voices spilled out – mostly Gaunt going on about the fine views of the surrounding hills. We hurried on up to the second floor, pushed open the door of the guest's room, and there was Mrs Buchan, puffing up a pillow.

She looked me up and down, then gave a little nod of approval seeing me wearing the terrible suit. "It'll do, I suppose," she snapped. "Now then Blackie, this room needs warmed. Can't you smell the damp in the air? A roaring fire is what it needs." She tutted when she saw that Frank was going to help me. She carried on sighing and smoothing down the bed sheets, as Frank kneeled on the floor by the fireplace.

I couldn't help staring at Mrs Buchan, who had her hair up in a tight bun. She looked about fifty, and fed up. And Elsie said she wasn't married. All housekeepers are called 'Mrs'. I wanted to ask her about John Hogg and the deeds of the house. I did open my mouth. I did get as far as muttering, "Um, Mrs Buchan…" But she just scowled at me.

"Don't stand there like you've been struck by lightning. If you can't make the fire yourself, at least dust the mantelpiece. Lord knows I've been at it for hours, sewing up bed sheets, pummelling the mattress and airing blankets. And Frank, tell that no-good sister of yours the guest will need a jug of water by the bed, and a glass. A *clean* glass, mind." Then her beady eyes were back on me. She saw my bare and manky feet. "Lord above," she sighed then marched round the bed, pulled out a cloth from her belt and shoved it into my hands. "Wipe the soles of your clarty feet. Then see to it that Elsie finds you clogs." She sighed again. "Standards have sorely slipped. I have seen to the bed.

You see to the rest." Then, glancing about the room and shaking her head, she strode out.

"The deeds of the house," I mumbled, but she was already stomping along the corridor. Behind me I heard a crackle in the fire grate.

"Mr Hogg tucked them away somewhere safe, so word goes, and couldna remember where." I swung round to stare at Frank, who was now bathed in an orange flickering glow. "I've a notion they could be hidden in the secret passage."

I looked at him.

"Awesome," I said.

Frank just screwed up his orange face, like I was talking a foreign language.

"Is there really a secret passage?" I asked, and was about to say, 'Cool!' but changed it to, "Cor! Sounds handy."

He shrugged and poked the fire. "Or, p'rhaps he stuffed them in a tin along with the broken biscuits." He grinned. "Or tied them wi' red ribbon and put them in a drawer with his underwear and mothballs!"

He winked at me, then stood up, his perfect fire roaring away in the big stone fireplace.

"Don't I get as much as a 'Thank you kindly' for saving your bacon?" he asked, nodding to his fire. "You're no better than the American."

"Totally, yeah, thanks Frank. That's great. Appreciate it. Really."

Just then we heard voices out on the landing. It sounded as though Gaunt and the very important guest were heading upstairs. "You will have total privacy here, Mr Inglis. No one will disturb you," I heard Gaunt say loudly, like he wanted us to hear. There were grubby footprints on the floor and ash scattered about. If this was a hotel, I thought, it wasn't even one-star. Frank grabbed my elbow and the coal bucket and steered me out of the room into the corridor.

"We don't want to bump into his majesty, do we?" he mumbled, but I couldn't see how we could avoid it. The footsteps were growing louder and heading our way. At the end of the gas-lit corridor was what looked like a full-length, wonky mirror. With the footsteps coming to the top of the stairs, Frank pushed the mirror – and it opened. "This way," he whispered and stepped into the darkness. Something told me I was about to discover the secret passage. Suddenly it didn't feel so awesome. Frank grabbed my arm and pulled me into a dark cupboard – again! The mirror door swung shut behind us.

"That's better," he whispered. "Out of harm's way, eh?"

I felt panic. It wasn't just me jammed in some wee cupboard this time – there were two of us, and the truth was Frank didn't smell the best. I tried not to breathe. I couldn't tell whether my eyes were shut or not, it was that pitch black.

"Here we go then," whispered Frank and, next thing, I had more space. My elbow wasn't up against Frank's shoulder. My legs weren't pressed against the coal bucket. I heard another door creak open. Foul-smelling air hit my nostrils. "This way," said Frank. There was some kind of door at the back of the cupboard, leading into a passage. There was nothing else for it, so I followed.

25

Frank led the way with me hanging on behind. He suddenly stopped and I banged my nose against the back of his head.

"Steps ahead," he announced. "Take care." Steps? They were more like cliffs, or three steps in one. They wound round and round and were so steep you had to practically jump down them, which, in the pitch black when you are trying to be as quiet as a mouse, and your nose is throbbing, wasn't easy. Without much hope I patted the cold walls for hidden title deeds.

The last few steps were wooden, not stone, I guessed, because they echoed more. At the bottom was a low, narrow tunnel. I kept hold of the edge of Frank's jacket. I felt like a baby on reins. "Frank?" I whispered, though probably I could have shouted and nobody would hear. The walls were that thick.

"What?" He kept shuffling along and I kept shuffling right behind, the coal bucket clattering against the wall.

"Why do you put up with all this? I mean, why don't you run away?"

"And starve tae death? Gaunt wouldna gie us a character. We wouldna find another place. And p'rhaps you havena noticed, but Elsie wouldna last two days sleeping under the stars and foraging for berries and begging for scraps. As it is, she can barely carry out her duties. As long as she needs me I'm not going nowhere." Then he stopped and I bumped into him again. "I know it's no up tae much, but it's a job." He took in a fast snatch of breath. "And Gaunt will get his comeuppance."

We carried on inching along in silence, images of Gaunt's comeuppance flashing through my head. Gaunt thrown off a horse. Gaunt drowning in mud in the trenches. Gaunt with a bayonet stuck through his chest. Gaunt choking on poisoned porridge. I decided we must be underground. It seemed forever we were in that secret passageway. I thought how, when Agnes and I got back to our time, we would try and find this again with Will and Robbie. If it hadn't fallen in.

"I think we're nearly there, thank God," Frank whispered, loudly. We had come up some steep stone steps again. "It's somewhere round here," he said, fumbling. I stretched out my hand and hit what felt like wood. We had reached another door.

I had this mad hope that through that door was Mum and Dad and the twins and bright lights and a TV, and my stuff and normal food, and all I had to do was push it open and everything would be back the way it was. Frank could join the gang. He'd love it. And he could go to Peebles High School with Agnes and me.

Frank turned the handle. I gasped at the thunderous creaking noise. He stopped. We huddled in the dark, waiting for Gaunt to discover us. But there was nothing. Not a sound. So Frank pushed again and we piled through into a cupboard, a bit like the one we had started in. 'Clever', I thought to myself, figuring out how the secret passageway worked.

"We're in the boot room," Frank said. "Watch out for the dead hare hanging up. I trapped it myself."

I turned a fraction and something furry brushed against my cheek. Gross!

I bit my tongue so I wouldn't yell out, and next thing Frank turned another handle, the door of the boot room opened and we were back in the dreary kitchen. Elsie was in her little recess bed next to the range. On the table one candle burned. Frank dropped the bucket, took off his cap, padded over to the sideboard and lifted the huge kettle.

He looked at me and grinned, "A cup o' tea, Saul?" He looked exhausted.

"I'll no say no to a cup o' tea." That was Elsie. I'd thought she was asleep.

So had Frank apparently, because he told her so.

"Don't like to sleep afore you're back safe and sound," she said.

"Well, I'm back. And so is he. And the blooming American is in his room and you were to put a jug o' water by his bed." Elsie threw back her grey blanket with a mutter but Frank held up his hand. "Back to bed. Nobody's running out to the pipe to fetch water now and there's precious little here for our tea. We can let him know what thirst is, eh?"

Elsie giggled and pulled the blanket up to her pointy little chin, her straggly hair spilling down around her small face.

Frank set the kettle over the gas flame. "Then once we've had our cup o' tea we can all bed down. For daresay his blinking majesty will be shaking us up at dawn to wait on his fancy guest. We'll be at his beck and call, you wait. We'll have to bat away his stinking farts."

Elsie giggled again. "Aye, and pick his blooming fat nose."

"And stoop to lift his dropped silken handkerchiefs," went on Frank, acting it out. They were on a roll now. My head swivelled from Frank to Elsie, like I was at a tennis match.

"They're all the same, the gentry. They blooming well drop them on purpose just to see us stoop."

"And then they ring a bell for us tae rise in the middle o' the night tae shoo mice fae their bed chamber."

"Or a bumble bee." Elsie batted the air.

"Or a spider." Frank pinched a finger and thumb together, and put on a terrified face, like he was transporting a tarantula.

"And carry heavy parcels, our eyes cast down. Oh, sometimes," Elsie wrung her little hands together and sighed, "I could fair weep at all the blinkin' work."

"Well, Mr America won't know where his famous Scots porridge has been, will he?" At that Frank spat on the ground. "Gaunt never guesses."

I nodded like I knew what they were talking about. Did they mix Gaunt's porridge with a bit of horse poo before serving it up to him?

I had gone off my cup of tea, but I drank it. Like Mrs Buchan said, standards were dropping, mine included.

I was worn out and feeling sorry for myself at the end of a long day, and I must have looked it, because just before I went to lie down under my scratchy woollen blanket, Elsie came and gave me a sympathetic pat on the shoulder. "Poor orphan laddie. But at least now yea're better dressed."

I muttered a reluctant thanks. What a joke! I had never been worse dressed in my life.

"There, there, laddie," she went on. "Lord knows it's hard when there's nobody in the world coming to knock on the door looking for yea."

But as it turned out, Elsie was wrong. Someone did come knocking at the door.

26

Agnes Brown came knocking at the door, which is how we both ended up working in Gaunt House on August 4th, 1914, the day Britain entered the First World War.

"Just for a few days, to tide us over, mind," Mrs Buchan said, handing Elsie's black dress, white apron and white cap to Agnes. "And you, missy," she said, firing her words in Elsie's direction, "take three days in your bed to get your strength back. And thank your stars another scullery maid appeared like a blessed angel." Then the housekeeper glared at Frank, me and Agnes, all lined up like naughty school kids in the dreary kitchen. Agnes curtsied, which I thought was a bit over the top. Mrs Buchan pointed to the ceiling. "We've a very important guest to see to. Has he stirred yet?"

Me and Frank shook our heads. "Gaunt wants everything just so. He'll need the fire seen to." She said that to me. I nodded, wondering if I should salute or bow. "Yes. Mrs. Buchan," she said to me, in a spelling-out kind of way.

I could feel my face turning red. "Yes, Mrs Buchan."

Then she scowled at Agnes. "You can fetch water then set it to boil. Now that the cook's gone 'tis myself expected to turn out a meal. You can fetch in potatoes, scrub and peel them. Mr Lamb leaves them by the back door."

"Yes, Mrs Buchan," Agnes said, not needing any prompt. She already had the funny white cap on. I bet she couldn't wait to get into the clothes she was holding. For Agnes Brown, it was like we were in a play. By this time Mrs Buchan was dealing with Frank.

"You, Noble, once you've cleaned Gaunt's boots and skinned that hare, can go into town." I could see Frank standing up straighter, trying not to grin. He'd already told me how running errands was the highlight of his job. "It seems our American guest wishes a… bicycle."

Elsie tittered from her recess bed.

"It's no laughing matter, Elsie Noble," Mrs Buchan snapped. She turned back to Frank. "Go to Scott Brothers on the High Street and tell them you require a sturdy gentlemen's bicycle."

Bikes were *my* thing. I knew everything about bikes. "Please, Mrs Buchan," I blurted out, "can I go with him?" She glared at me. She saw me as the dirty coat thief. "I mean… I know a lot about bikes. I can help Frank choose a good one." She stared at me like I was mad. "I mean, I can make sure he doesn't get cheated."

Frank cottoned-on quick. "Aye, Mrs Buchan. I could do wi' a knowing eye. There's all sorts of bicycles nowadays: sturdy ones, and shoddy ones too."

"And… I know the difference," I said, smiling at her, trying hard to shake off my low-life image.

"Course, I know all there is tae know about horses,"

Frank said, "but the bicycle is a very different matter, Mrs Buchan."

Mrs Buchan looked from me to Frank and back to me, but I could tell by the glazed look in her eyes and the way her shoulders slumped that she was past caring. I pictured her in days gone by, a hard-working housekeeper making order in a big, busy, comfortable house. I even imagined her singing in her work, but not now.

"Oh, very well then," she said with a sigh, "but look smart about it. It's to go on Mr Gaunt's account. And make sure it is a bicycle fit for a gentleman. The guest plans on taking an excursion tomorrow, so I'm told." Then she raised her eyebrows like she didn't approve, clapped her hands and we were off. Agnes wriggled into her maid's outfit. Frank went to skin a hare and I scarpered off to the coal shed. I was going to buy a hundred-year-old bike. How cool was that! I practically skipped on the cobbles, which is pretty tricky when you've got blisters and are wearing heavy clogs. Maybe it was also because me and Agnes were together again, but suddenly I felt much happier.

Agnes hadn't been in the house five minutes before she was on about the deeds. "They're not in the kitchen," she told me, "nor near the water-pipe." We were walking back over the courtyard together, towards the back door, me swinging my bucket of coal – was there less coal today or was I growing stronger? – and Agnes with her big pail of water sloshing around. "What about the privy, Saul?" Agnes giggled. "You know the smelly outdoor loo? Have you checked in there?"

The truth was I hadn't. Who would put important documents in a privy? "You can borrow my torch next time you go," she said, "and when you're in the rooms doing the fires have a good rummage."

"I have," I whispered, slowing down as we approached the back door. "I've searched down the back of armchairs, under beds, in drawers. Nothing."

Above us I heard a creaking noise. I glanced up and there was the mysterious important guest, sticking his head out the window. Bold Agnes, probably not knowing how servants were supposed to be not seen, not heard, shouted up, "Welcome to Scotland. Are you enjoying it so far?"

The American looked stunned. "Oh, ah, yes, yes. It does seem a very… ah, peaceful spot," he stammered before disappearing back inside. It struck me again that he had a strange American accent. There was something not quite right about it.

But there wasn't time to worry about that. I lugged the heavy bucket along the dim corridor and Agnes bustled off to the kitchen.

"If you see the master or his guest on the stair, give room." That was the advice from Frank and here I was, stepping to the side, looking down at my daft clogs while his American majesty swept by. He didn't even mutter 'good morning', 'or afternoon', or whatever time of the day it was. When he was past, I carried on, hurrying now. I didn't know how much time I had. My heart was pounding and not only from lugging the coal. I was going to search in his room for deeds, papers, anything I could lay my hands on.

I slipped in. He had made his bed. The room looked way better than it had last night. All very neat. Must be a tidy sort of guy. A pair of grey socks lay folded on the one chair and a grey jacket lay draped over the back of it. With my heart pounding I fumbled in the pockets of the jacket. My eyes fell on a label inside the jacket: –

Schmidt von Stuttgart

And in the pocket I felt a coin, large, like a twenty-first-century two-pound coin. I glanced at it. It was foreign, that was for sure, but I didn't know from where. I shoved it into my own pocket so I could find out more. Then I hurried over to the fire and swept out the ash. My eyes darted everywhere: under the bed, along shelves, the mantelpiece. I couldn't see any suspicious papers lying around. I stacked a few twigs then tried to light them. My hands shook so much the match went out, but the next one worked. I threw on a stub of candle wax that Frank had given me. It flared up. Maybe it was the flames filling me with courage, but after I put on a few coals I started rummaging.

There was a large leather bag next to the bed. It seemed totally unlikely that the deeds of this house were stashed away in the bag of the American guest, but there was something about him that didn't make sense, and I wanted to look everywhere. Deep in the bag, among what felt like silk shirts, I brushed paper. By this time I could hear footsteps on the stairs. I pulled the paper out and stuffed it in my pocket without even looking at it, then ran back to heap more coals on the fire. The footsteps on the stairs were getting closer. I snatched up my now empty bucket and walked out as casually as I could, my eyes down as I passed the important guest going back to his room.

27

"She's a proper angel, your sister," Elsie said, soon as I opened the kitchen door. Agnes flashed me that don't-say-anything look. Her and Elsie were hunched over the kitchen table, Agnes now looking like the little maid and Elsie like a patient, with her old baggy nightdress on and a ragged tartan shawl draped over her thin shoulders. There was a jar on the table with buttercups in it that brightened the place up. Agnes and Elsie were huddled over an upturned teacup. Elsie carefully took the cup then turned it back the right way.

"On yea go then," she whispered to Agnes, "read my fortune, but if it's bad don't tell me."

"It all seems… lovely," Agnes said, way too fast for a fortune-teller.

I felt sorry for Elsie. She was so eager and pleased. Whichever way you looked at it, her future was bound to be bad. If it wasn't her cough it was the war. Ill health and death hung over her like a black cloud.

"Hey, Agnes," I interrupted, "I need to show you something." I beckoned for her to follow me outside. Next thing we were whispering at the back door.

"I found something," I said, pulling the piece of

paper from the guest's bag out of my pocket. I fished out the coin too. "And this," I said, gazing at it properly, "looks old, and, um, foreign."

We both glanced at the penny, or whatever it was, but neither of us could work out where it was from. Agnes peered at the paper as I unfolded it; we were both nervously glancing about. "It's a map," she whispered. "That's not the deeds. We're looking for old papers, handwritten, signed by a solicitor or lawyer, and with John Hogg's signature on." Agnes smoothed down her apron. "I have been cleaning the kitchen. Did you notice? I've been working so hard."

It had seemed brighter. "Nice," I muttered.

"Thanks. Anyway, as I was cleaning I searched from roof to floor and didn't find a thing." While she was telling me this I had a look at the foreign guest's map. The Firth of Forth, Leith Docks, Edinburgh. Ships. The navy. And little red crosses marked here and there. I folded it up and shoved it back in my pocket. "Tourists always carry maps," Agnes whispered.

A map of Leith Docks? Seemed odd. Just then Frank came running from the stables, flinging his cap in the air.

"Time to purchase a bicycle," he whooped, waving the key for the gate in front of my eyes. "Come along then – you, the expert in two-wheeled conveyances!"

"Can I come too?" Agnes asked, jumping up and down. "I've cleaned the kitchen, polished the cutlery, and the glasses, mended a rip in a jacket and folded the laundry."

Frank's eyes grew wide. "Oh," Agnes went on, "and

I fetched water, heated it up and gave Elsie a little footbath. It did her the world of good." Frank shook his head in disbelief. "Please," Agnes pleaded, "can I come?"

Then Frank grinned at her. "Drape a shawl about your shoulders then tell Mrs Buchan you're clean out of salt. She's in the parlour."

Agnes dashed off to spin the salt lie.

"We'll have ourselves a ball," Frank said, tapping his finger to his nose like we were on some top-secret mission. "Our American guest," Frank pointed up to the second floor, "asks that his bicycle be oiled and prepared for two o'clock this afternoon." Frank whipped out an old-looking pocket watch. "Which gives us two hours." Then he rubbed his hands together, just like a wee kid on Christmas morning.

Agnes reappeared with a tartan blanket over her shoulders, giving us the thumbs up. "Mrs Buchan says it's an ill omen to have a kitchen without salt. And Elsie's fine," she said to Frank. "She's resting happily." Then we were off, Agnes practically skipping along.

I wished I had a camera. Even by 1914 standards I bet we looked pretty shabby. We all had patches stitched onto our clothes at the elbows and knees. Agnes's skirt looked like it had a whole bit added at the bottom.

We passed people in the lanes who didn't look shabby like we did. Frank kept taking off his cap and telling everyone we were off to buy a bicycle, like it was a Porsche or something.

"You don't say the mill manager is putting his hand in his pocket?" one man with a very bushy beard said.

"Hope Gaunt takes a tumble," said another man next to him, who then spat on the ground.

"And dies," hissed another. They were all leaning against a wall, smoking pipes and looking like they had all the time in the world.

"The bicycle is no for Gaunt," Frank piped up. "It's for our American guest," and he clicked his heels together, as though that is what Americans did. The men laughed.

Later, as we hurried along the High Street Frank told us these men had been mill workers but since Gaunt came along with his money-saving schemes he'd laid several workers off. "They cost too much, see?" Frank explained.

"Like the footman and the cook at the house," I said.

"Exactly."

Agnes's head was on a swivel. Even though the buildings in the town weren't much different from what we knew, the shops in them were completely different.

She read out the sign on what will become a boring old bank branch in the twenty-first century.

BOOK BINDING AND PRINTING

"Hosier," she said next, "whatever that means, oh, and clothiers."

"Ah!" Frank shouted. "That's what we're looking for: Scott Brothers," and at the same time he was doffing his cap to a lady in a wide-brimmed hat. When the lady had swept by, he pointed across the car-less street and I saw the words

ROYAL CAMPBELL CYCLES

next door to a shop where, back in my real life, Mum and Dad sometimes get Indian takeaway. He dashed over and we followed him.

We trouped into this big, dimly lit shop and I couldn't believe the amount of bikes in there. "It is the new horse," the shopkeeper said. I could have stayed for hours checking them all out. They were all heavy and black. Brand new but totally old fashioned. Some had no gears and no brakes. Some had really simple brakes, and the newest ones had three gears.

Some names on the bikes I recognised, like Raleigh and Triumph. There was one called Dursley-Pederson, but the best-looking bike was called 'Sunbeam'.

"It must be sturdy, Mr Scott," Frank said, while Agnes gazed about wide-eyed and I ran from bike to bike checking on spokes and chains and saddles. "And fit for a gentleman." The saddles were hard leather with huge springs under them. The frames weighed a ton.

The shopkeeper waved in the direction of the most expensive bike. It was the one I liked best. "The all-black three-speed Royal Sunbeam for gentlemen," he quoted, "with hand-applied rim brakes. A bargain for fifteen pounds, four shillings and sixpence." Frank looked like he was going to keel over. The shopkeeper didn't bat an eyelid. I nudged Frank and nodded at the Sunbeam.

"It's a beauty," I said.

"And sturdy," Agnes added. Frank looked on amazed as I wheeled the big bike out.

"Aye, fine," the shopkeeper said, waving us out the shop. "I'll add it to Gaunt's account."

We stepped out the shop and suddenly the church bells started to go mad. This wasn't like they were chiming the hour of the day, or some tinkling Christmas carol. This was urgent clanging. Everyone was surging up the High Street towards the church. Horses neighed. Children cried. People shouted. Dogs barked. People were pushing past and bumping into me.

"You know what this is, don't you, Saul?" Agnes said, grabbing hold of my arm in case we got separated. I wheeled the bike into the crowd.

The **CLANG-CLANG** of the bells slowed down. The crowd jostled to get near the front of the church. The horses stopped whinnying. The children stopped crying. The last bell tolled, then a hush fell over the crowd. A man in a big top hat came out and stood at the top of the stone steps.

"Ladies and gentlemen, girls and boys," his voice

boomed out, serious and slow. "It is my duty to inform you that today..." he paused and took a deep breath, "...today Britain has declared war on Germany." A gasp ran around the crowd. "We are at war," he announced.

28

In front of the church, the crowd jostled, taking in the news. People murmured, then the silence erupted.

"Our lads will teach them a lesson!" a woman shouted, and a few people cheered.

"There are tents to be erected on the green," the man in the top hat announced, "for men to join his majesty's regiments to let the Kaiser know that the glorious British Empire will come to the aid of Belgium."

More cheers from the crowd.

"It'll be over by Christmas!" someone shouted.

"Watch out for the enemy in our midst," said the man in the top hat, and everyone glanced over their shoulders. A few people stared at me and Agnes. We were strangers. Maybe they thought we were spies?

Next thing, the minister appeared at the door of the church and held up his hand. The crowd quietened down. "At a time such as this," he said, "let us pray." And the crowd bowed their heads. Men whipped off their caps. People clasped their hands together.

"Our Father," over a hundred people murmured all together, "which art in heaven…"

They had just said 'Amen', when I felt this tapping on my shoulder. I swung round and nearly dropped the bike. There was the woman we'd seen when we were busking. She had a white rose in her hair again, and she was smiling at me.

"Saul Martin, I presume?"

"It's my Auntie Jean," Agnes cried, giving the woman a hug.

"Hello," I mumbled and because I couldn't think what else to say, I tugged at Frank's sleeve. "Um, this is Frank Noble," I said. "He's a... a stable—"

"Soldier," Frank said, giving the woman a salute.

"Don't, Frank." Agnes looked like she would burst into tears. "Don't be a soldier."

"But, you are too young, surely?" the woman said.

"Haven't got no birth certificate," Frank said and I saw how he lifted his heels off the ground. "I can be whatever age the army needs me to be." Then he crumpled a bit, as if he'd suddenly remembered a problem. "First I need to see that Elsie is recovered. Then I'm off. Try and stop me. We need to do our duty." Then he turned to me, his dark eyes blazing. "What about you Saul? Surely you want to do your bit?"

I was only thirteen! What did he expect? Sometimes I'd wondered if he was thirteen too. It was hard to tell. Children in the past looked different. But mostly he seemed older than Elsie, and she was fourteen. I looked down at the bike and didn't answer him.

"But it'll all be over by Christmas," the woman said, "isn't that what they are telling us?"

Frank shrugged.

Agnes shook her head. The crowd was breaking up. "It will go on for four years," Agnes said. The woman looked sad. Frank, I thought, looked hopeful. He really wanted to go, I could tell. The only reason he wasn't running to the green to queue up was Elsie and her coughing.

Jean fumbled in the large pocket of her apron and brought out three red apples. "Eat while you may," she said, handing one to Agnes, one to Frank and one to me. But I needed both hands to steer the bike so I pocketed the apple. It rustled against the map in my pocket, which made me think about the guest, and getting the bike back for two o'clock. Jean took the white rose out of her hair and gave it to Agnes. "Be happy while you may," she said, "for something tells me nothing will ever be quite the same again." Then she gazed right into my eyes, like she knew we were time travellers and it didn't faze her. "I am very glad to have met you, Saul," she said, then nodded to Frank and smiled. "You too, Frank, and send my regards to your sister. I hope I have the pleasure of meeting her, and of meeting you again."

Then Agnes's great-great-great-great Auntie Jean turned and walked away. When she reached the turn in the road she stopped, turned her head and waved to us. The three of us waved back and while we were waving Agnes said, without looking round at Frank, "Jean said, Frank, that you and Elsie can go and live with her. She said she would be very happy about that. You can help with the garden, Frank, and Elsie can help around the house, and Jean knows about nursing, and making people better. She has two extra beds. She really means it."

Frank didn't say anything but I shot a look at him. He was pressing his lips together like he was trying not to cry.

He saw me, whipped out his pocket watch and snapped it open. "We better get our skates on," he said.

"Or bicycle," said Agnes.

I couldn't resist getting on the gentleman's Sunbeam bike and pedalling it along the High Street and up the lane with Frank and Agnes running along beside me. I changed the gears. I checked the brakes. I couldn't reach the leather saddle but I rode on the crossbar. What a brilliant bike! As Elsie would say, it was a lark! I wished I could cycle right into the twenty-first century. Check this out, Robbie, a 1914 Royal Sunbeam!

Gaunt was pacing about round the courtyard when we got back. "We stopped to hear the news, sir," Frank blurted out, before Gaunt had a chance to roar at us. "There's a war on, sir. We are at war with Germany."

I wheeled the heavy bike over the cobbles and Agnes darted back into the kitchen muttering something about peeling tatties.

"It has come then, as we all suspected," Gaunt said, thrusting his big hands onto his hips. He curled up his thick lips – and smiled! "The regiments will be needing khaki, reams of the stuff. Battalions of khaki. The mills will be working, twenty to the dozen, day and night."

"Um, the bicycle, sir?" I mumbled, not knowing what to do with it.

"Yes, the bicycle. See it is left by the front door." Now it was Gaunt inspecting his pocket watch. "This very instant, and make sure you leave no grubby fingerprints on the handles. And remember, our important guest does not wish to be disturbed." Then he pointed to the house, "Clean the windows, Blackie, you hear? Crack at it!"

"Yes, sir," I muttered and then it was me chewing my lip and trying not to smile, thinking how a window cleaner got a good chance to peer into rooms and see things.

I left the bike leaning against the stone wall of the house, next to the front door. It had no stand. In the distance I could hear the church bells chime for two o'clock. Same bells that had clanged the news of war were back to their usual job of telling the time. The front door opened. I nipped round the side of the house and hid. Mr Inglis was punctual, that was for sure. I pressed against the wall and with one eye spied the American guest trying to mount the bike. He wobbled a bit as he rode it in a circle in front of the house. The thick front tyre must have hit a stone or something because he wobbled again, then he and the bike keeled over and he hissed under his breath, "*Gott im Himmel!*" Which I thought was a funny thing for an American to say. We had done a term of German at school and I wasn't bad at it. Those were definitely German words: 'God in heaven'.

I felt a shiver run up the back of my neck. I'd always had a hunch there was something dodgy about this 'guest'. I remembered the label of his jacket. Stuttgart was in Germany; I knew that because they had a football team. Why would an American buy a jacket from Germany? My heart skipped a beat. And there was something fishy about him having a map of Leith Docks.

The guest brushed down his trousers, got on the bike again and was off. I could hear Gaunt open the gate for him. "Bad news I'm afraid," Gaunt bellowed, "it would seem we are at war." Then he said something about the pleasant leafy lanes of Peebles.

It was a good time for me to do a spot of window cleaning, and I knew just whose room I was going to start with.

29

I dashed into the kitchen for a window-cleaning cloth and some water. There was Agnes sitting on Elsie's bed holding her hand and telling her, I guessed, about her Auntie Jean: "And there are red geraniums at the window. It is so pretty. And she makes brews from herbs and plants to cure all sorts of bad coughs." Elsie, by the way she was gazing into Agnes's eyes, looked like her wishes were coming true.

I had planned on telling Agnes my hunches about our mysterious American, but now didn't seem like the time. "Gaunt wants me to clean the windows," I said instead.

"Use vinegar and old newspapers," Elsie called over. "You'll find them in the cupboard behind that old mirror. Just gie it a shove with your shoulder and abracadabra, it'll open."

Amazingly, it did! Agnes was gaping. I knew what she was thinking. She had searched the kitchen all over – but I bet she never found this secret cupboard! Right enough, the cupboard was jammed full of old newspapers. "I heard Hogg was a terrible hoarder with newspapers," Elsie chirped. She was right about that, even by 1914 standards, they were ancient. Yellowing crinkled paper fell out. One said:

BORDER CRIER
MARCH 16ᵀᴴ 1893

Agnes ran over to where I was stuffing the newspapers back into the secret cupboard. "I thought," she said, gasping and shaking her head, "that this was just an old mirror." She scooped up some of the newspapers and started flicking through them.

"It's not the *only* secret cupboard in this house," I told her, as I grabbed a random newspaper and found a bottle of vinegar. "Come upstairs and I'll show you another one." She was up like a shot. "This one has a secret passage," I explained as we slipped through the house. "Yeah, no joke! Actually, it was where Frank thought old Hogg would have hidden the deeds."

"Really?!" Agnes's eyes were intent.

"Yeah, we both had a fumble about but didn't come across anything," We were heading up the stairs. "It's pitch black in there, you can't see a thing. I warn you, Agnes, it's pretty scary."

"Wait!" Agnes grabbed my arm. "I'll be back in a second; I'm going to get my torch. It's under my pillow."

She was back right away and we sped quietly upstairs. I left my vinegar and newspapers by the visitor's door, and showed Agnes the wonky mirror in the hallway. I pressed it with my shoulder, and we stepped into the secret cupboard.

It didn't feel as creepy when it was all lit up with good twenty-first-century technology. The door at the back was easy to see. We stepped through to the steep circular stone stairs.

"Wow!" said Agnes, flashing her torch all over the low narrow passage.

It was cool, a secret stairway, but it was all just bare stone. Dusty as anything and slightly damp, but nowhere you could hide stuff. We crept down, hearing our own breathing and our footsteps down the stone and wooden stairs. We looked all along the underground passage to the boot room door. Nothing.

Agnes hung her head. She really really wanted to find those deeds.

"I better do the windows," I said, and was going to go back to my duties on the second floor.

"If I was John Hogg," said Agnes, "I would have thought this was a great hiding place. I bet only the servants know it exists. Gaunt wouldn't know. He's never in the cupboards or the boot room. Let me just think…" She turned and looked back along the underground passage to the bottom of the spiral stairs. "Saul!" she said, her voice lifting, "Why are these last steps wooden, do you think?"

I knelt down and tapped them and looked more closely. What a difference it made, searching with light.

Agnes sunk to her knees too and felt along under a thicker board. "Saul! I think it's a hinge. Have you still got that weird coin? Maybe we can lever it in under here." We did, and amazingly the middle wooden step lifted like a lid.

30

Agnes gasped. The torchlight lurched. So I held the torch steady while she slipped her hand under the step. "There's something in here," she whispered, "something small." I trained the light close and saw her pull out a small iron key. A tag on the key said:

John Robert Hogg, Esq.

"It's his! But what does it open?" Agnes held it up in the torchlight. We looked and felt all around the steps, all along the passage again, but there was no sign of a box or trunk or secret door. We had a key, but we didn't know what for. I didn't know whether to be glad or not. By the look of her, neither did Agnes. She shrugged and gazed at me quizzically.

"We better stop looking now, Agnes," I said. I needed to get on with cleaning the windows. "Hey! We've got a key. That's great." I tried to sound upbeat. "All we need now is a lock."

We crept back through the boot room. Elsie was napping, no one was around; the visitor was still out on his bicycle. Agnes, with the mysterious key safe in her pocket, when off to chop cabbage while I bounded up the main staircase to my vinegar and newspapers. I wanted to do some investigating while I had the chance. I didn't know how long the 'American' would be gone. Maybe I was totally wrong, but something told me Mr Inglis wasn't really American, and probably wasn't called Mr Inglis either. I was up the stairs and in his room in no time. That was a good thing about being a servant: servants knew things! They went into other people's rooms, they changed beds, made fires, set out jugs of water, cleaned windows!

From his window I had a clear view down the front driveway to the gate. Plus the huge iron gates were creaky. I would hear him coming. I slipped the map of Leith Docks back to the bottom of his leather bag then pulled open drawers. I flung off blankets and felt about under the mattress, under the pillow. I patted under the rugs. I hit around the walls for any more secret cupboards. But I didn't find anything.

Feeling a bit of an idiot, I made the bed and tried to put everything back the way it had been. Maybe I'd been thinking in the wrong direction. Why would a German spy come to Peebles anyway?

Just when I'd decided I should really crack on with the window cleaning, I spied a brown envelope sticking out of the grey Stuttgart-labelled jacket that was folded neatly over the chair. My heart raced. Hardly thinking what I was doing I pulled it out. It was addressed to some person in Sweden. I thought about peeling it open then and there, but it was sealed at the back with white candle wax. I dashed over to the window. There was still no sign of him, or Gaunt who I was pretty sure was down at the mill getting ready to make big dosh from the war.

I bolted down into Gaunt's study, rifled through his writing desk, grabbed a brown envelope and fountain pen and, with shaking hands, managed to copy the writing of the address. It looked almost the same. Then I ran back to the guest's room, ripped a sheet from the newspaper and slipped that into the envelope. Now all I needed was a bit of candle wax and that was easy enough. There were candles everywhere. I struck a match, held it under the wax till a bit dripped on the back of the envelope. It hardened and that was it sealed. Then I swapped the letters, slipping the one I had made into the jacket pocket on the chair. I grabbed the vinegar and what was left of the old newspaper and hurried out of the room. With my heart banging like a drum, I softly closed the door behind me.

Then I really did clean windows, loads of them, as the sun got lower. The strong smell of hare stew wafted through the house and the letter to Sweden waited in my pocket. The old newspapers I was cleaning with had adverts trying to get people to go and live in America! And adverts for Scotch whisky, and Edinburgh Rock.

From a window on the landing I saw Frank down by the stables with a pole slung across his shoulders, rifle style, marching back and forth over the cobbles. I knew what he was getting in training for. From another window I saw the gardener sitting on a log smoking a pipe. Then from the library window I saw the American (who by now I was convinced wasn't American) cycling up the driveway. He swung off the bike and there was Gaunt, slapping his thighs and offering his guest a sherry in the drawing room, and there was Frank, running to take the bike like it was a horse. I wondered if he was going to put it in the stable?

By this time, twenty windows done, my arms were aching. I was onto my last scrap of newspaper and was about to scrunch it up and soak it with vinegar when I saw someone had circled an article in ink. It read:

BURIED TREASURE

A VERITABLE treasure trove was recently discovered in Melrose, under a yew tree. After considerable examination, detectives and scholars suggest the box of rubies was put in the earth for safe keeping in the last part of the sixteenth century. The roots of the yew hold fast…

I felt my palms sweat. Someone – Mr Hogg I guessed – had given this article special attention. The same Mr Hogg who had also carefully drawn and painted the yew and its roots and stored the pictures in his treasure chest. Mr Hogg who, Agnes said, called this place 'Yew Tree House'.

My heart was racing. Suddenly it hit me. I *knew* where the deeds were! Everything pointed to it. They were in a very special place, sure enough. They were hidden under the yew tree! I wanted to shout out loud. With shaking fingers I put the circled newspaper article in my pocket, next to the letter to Sweden that was never going to Sweden.

"Agnes!" I belted along the corridor and burst into the kitchen. A candle was burning on the table. Elsie was sleeping in her recess bed by the stove and Agnes, dressed like a maid, cabbage all chopped, was knee-deep in old newspapers.

"History is fascinating," she said, holding up a paper with a photo of a bear. "Can you believe this, Saul?"

> ## *Harry the dancing bear delights the Beltane crowds in Peebles*

It looked like she had a whole stack of fascinating history to show me. "And this—"

"Agnes, listen," I burst out, hunching down next to her. "I think I know where the deeds are hidden, and I think we've got a German spy upstairs drinking sherry and pretending he's American!"

31

Agnes

Dear diary,

It is very late on August 4th, 1914, and I am far too excited to go to sleep. Anyway, head to toe in this little kitchen bed, with Elsie's feet (a bit smelly I must say) in my face plus her coughing, even if I wasn't too excited I don't think I could sleep. That was a very long sentence. And perhaps didn't make sense. The good news is that Frank sharpened my pencil, believe it or not, with a knife! So now it has ridged ends instead of smooth but I am so happy to have a sharp pencil I feel like writing all night. I am using my torch, which I am glad to say is still going strong.

But sharp pencils and torches are nothing compared with the really big news WHICH IS... we think we know where the deeds are. Just in case Gaunt snatches this diary, I am not actually going to write down where, but in the morning me and Saul are going to do a recce. Recce is from the word reconnaissance meaning 'To check things out'. It is an army word, which reminds me to say we were at a gathering outside the parish church when the actual news of the war was officially announced to the people. It was serious and scary and people kept pushing me and Saul was struggling to keep the crowds off the bike he had just got.

My great-great-great-great Auntie Jean is the nicest person in the whole world and because she is here in 1914 I feel hopeful. If the world was full of Gaunts I would not feel hopeful. But from what I can see, most people are friendly but they are scared of Mr Gaunt. Except not Jean. She isn't scared of him and when she says his name she spits on the ground, which seems really rude, but what I think is that people just did more spitting in the past.

I have left the biggest news till last. It makes my heart race just thinking about it. I can't bear thinking that I am under the same roof as a spy! I don't know how Saul can sleep. He said today felt like the busiest day of his whole life. Well, he deserves a good sleep because he is completely heroic. He actually worked out the code in the letter. It was so exciting. We scurried over to the privy, which is the name of the not-very-nice outside toilet — which is more or less a bucket in a shed. Anyway, privy means private, so if you are in there doing the toilet no one is supposed to disturb you. Saul tore open the envelope and I got out the torch. Then I thought how boring it was — a letter about the number of chimneys in the mansion house and a report on Scottish building styles and a list of trees in the garden. I thought our American guest was writing travel articles for Swedish magazines, but Saul, whispering so quiet I could hardly hear him said, I don't think so! Saul said the trees were the code names for types of ships, and the chimneys were numbers of fleets, and the building styles meant ages and sizes of ships and numbers of sailors and he said a bit about four lost meant four ships were being repaired in the docks. Seven out meant seven ships from the fleet were setting sail! I shook so much, the torch wobbled. I could never have worked out all that, but when Saul said it, I knew he was right. Saul also worked out that our phoney American was planning a long bike ride to Leith Docks the next day. When I asked him how he knew, he said he overheard the man asking Gaunt how long would it take to cycle to the port at Edinburgh and Gaunt told him if a trotting horse was similar to a bicycle, possibly four hours. The man said he would take his breakfast at nine and Saul said the man asked for smoked kippers instead of porridge!

Now that I have written all this down I think maybe I could fall asleep. Poor little Elsie has stopped fidgeting. Sometimes she lies so still I think she might be dead. I don't want her to die. I am so happy to have found my Auntie Jean. She is like a mother to me and I think she will be like a mother to Elsie. Maybe to Frank too. Though Frank says he will be a soldier and serve his country but I am going to tell him all the reasons why he shouldn t go. I hope I don t catch Elsie s cough. Jean says from my description it sounds like influenza. Now... I am... so sleepy.

3**2**

Amazing how well you can sleep on a hard bed with a scratchy blanket, but considering the war, never mind a spy on the second floor, plus the deeds to this land under our yew tree, I slept like I didn't have a care in the world.

I got up and saw that Frank's bed was empty. Gaunt, so Frank said, likes to get to the mill early, so no doubt Frank was up saddling his horse.

Pretty easy to get dressed in the morning when you never got undressed the night before. I didn't care if I looked a mess. This was the second day of the Great War and I was on a mission. I could hear Elsie coughing in the kitchen. I could hear Mrs Buchan clattering about, muttering about kippers and telling Agnes to set a pan of water on for tea. Next thing the housekeeper banged on my door. "You young servant, be getting the coals into the scuttles, you hear. High time you were up and at it."

I was up. Pretty soon I would be at it. "Yes, Mrs Buchan," I said, slipping my blistered feet into the clompy clogs then taking them out again. For my spy-catching plan, bare feet were better. I slunk out the back door then ran over to the stables. It looked like

Gaunt had already left. His horse had, and there was Frank with a big broom sweeping the dung aside. Like I thought, the bike was in the stables with bits of mud and hay sticking to the tyres.

"It's a bike, Frank," I said, "not a horse. The mud clogs the chain." Like I was suddenly feeling all responsible for this bike, which was funny considering how I was about to tamper with it.

"Keep yer hat on," Frank said. "Course I know that. I didn't know where to put the blinking thing, did I?" He went on sweeping up the dung and more specs of dirt splatted onto the new bike. I wheeled it outside and rubbed off the dirt with my sleeve. Frank had come to the stable door and was leaning on his broom, watching me. "I wis thinking," he said, "how you and me could take a wee wander down the green. See the tents going up. They're calling up the reservists for the King's Own Scottish Borderers. I thought – when the work's done – we could take a look."

I went on polishing the handlebars. I wasn't an expert on hundred-year-old bikes, but the mechanics looked pretty simple. The metal brake levers were attached to rods. These metal rods operated the front and back brakes. My mind raced. "Got a spanner?" I asked, casual like, "So I can check the wheel nuts." Frank looked impressed, like he'd never heard of wheel nuts, or rods, but he shook his head. There probably wasn't much need for a spanner in the stables. "Or pliers?" I said, lowering my voice. I reckoned pliers were old fashioned enough to have been invented. Thankfully he ran off and was back a minute later with an old pair of pliers.

Anybody watching from the house would think I was just polishing the handlebars. But I wasn't. I slightly loosened the holding nuts on the front and rear brakes, which were next to each other below the handlebars. If the phoney American pulled on the brakes going along a flat road they would work, but going down a hill where you need more pressure, they wouldn't. I slipped the pliers into my pocket.

"Frank?"

"Whit?"

"Where's the police station?" I asked him, running the duster along the heavy black frame.

"Down by the church. Why?"

"Could you go round there? Tell them there is an enemy alien who is going to cycle from Peebles to Leith Docks." I lifted my eyebrows, meaning the second floor, meaning our very own American guest.

"I wouldn't put n-n-nothing past Gaunt," Frank stammered. The poor guy had turned white.

"The spy is having breakfast at nine," I went on. "I'm to have this bike ready by the front door for him at half-past nine. Tell the police to be at the bottom of the steep road by the river," I lowered my voice, "two minutes after half-past nine. The corner where the road turns sharp onto the High Street. If my calculations are right, that is the first place he will slam on his brakes. Or... try to." Frank's eyes widened in amazement. "Then," I said, flicking the duster across the saddle, "he'll fall flat on his face."

I slipped my hand in my pocket and fished out the foreign coin and the coded letter. "Show them this. Tell them if they want to save the Royal Navy they better get a move on. I think the coin is German but I'm not sure. Oh, and Frank – leave the gate unlocked". Frank saluted me, slipped the letter in his pocket and ran off.

Whistling the latest Biffy Clyro song, I carefully wheeled the bike round to the front of the house. This time I didn't get on it. In the distance I heard the church bells chime for nine o'clock. The spy – because by now I was convinced that's what he was – would be munching kippers in the dining room right now. I ran back round to the kitchen where Agnes was washing dishes and Elsie was drinking tea and singing to herself.

"Mrs Buchan is serving him breakfast," Agnes whispered. Dripping soapsuds onto the floor, she pulled at my sleeve. "Let's run down to the yew tree now."

"The deeds aren't going anywhere, Agnes," I whispered. "They've been hidden for years. Trust me. They're not going to suddenly disappear." It felt like I'd been whispering for days. But Elsie didn't seem interested in what me and Agnes were up to. "And from what I know of time travel," I said, louder now, "we can't take anything with us. We'll get the deeds in 2014."

"So what about the key?" Agnes asked, patting her pocket. "If we can't take things with us, what are going to do with it?"

"We can hide it in the yew tree," I said, then I pulled her by the sleeve. "But right now, do you fancy seeing something way better than a dancing bear?"

"You bet," she said, drying her hands on her apron. She tied a shawl around her shoulders and said bye to Elsie.

"What'll I say to Mrs Buchan?" Elsie called.

"Tell her... um..."

"We've gone to buy you oranges," I said, and Elsie laughed and wheezed like oranges were precious jewels. I slipped into my clogs. It was time to catch a spy.

Thankfully Frank had remembered to leave the gate unlocked. Opening it slowly so it wouldn't creak, we slipped through, shut it, then ran as fast as we could into town. The church clock chimed for half-past nine. The spy would be opening the front door. Agnes and me hurried along the road. The spy would be swinging his leg over the bike. I hoped like mad he wouldn't test the brakes before he set off. Me and Agnes reached the market cross on the High Street. The spy would be pedalling along the flat track, away from the house. We ran to the corner of the High Street, to where the road swoops downhill from the bridge. On the pavement there was a man selling ice cream from a box. He had a horse tied up next to him. Agnes and I positioned ourselves beside him. I looked anxiously around for signs of policemen but couldn't see any. I glanced up at the church clock. It was already twenty-five minutes to ten. Maybe Frank hadn't told the police? Maybe the spy had taken another road? Or maybe he discovered the brakes were faulty? "They're saying they might have need of him," the ice cream man was saying, patting his old horse and looking really sad. "They're saying every good horse will be needed in the war." The horse shook its mane and the man fed it a scoop of ice cream. "Vanilla's her favourite," the man said, then he turned to a group of ladies strolling by. "Ices! Penny ices!

Delicious, mouth-watering, sweet on the tongue and all for a penny. Ices!"

I was so busy gaping up at this ice cream man and feeling sorry for his old horse that I practically missed the American guest cycling across the bridge.

"I think that's him!" Agnes grabbed me by the arm.

33

I saw him. The spy. He was gathering speed coming down the hill. His grey jacket was flapping out behind him. He was going to have to brake any moment to turn the corner. In a panic I looked about for signs of police. Where were they? The man on the bike sped to the corner. He was getting faster and faster. "He's trying to brake," Agnes said, sinking her fingers into my arm.

"Yeah," I said, "and he can't!" Sure enough the man on the bike stuck his legs out. I could see panic on his face. He was wobbling out of control. A tall man dressed in black stepped out of the crowd. He had a rounded black helmet on. From the other side of the street I saw another man dressed the same. Then another one ran out of the sweetie shop. The police were everywhere. Frank had done it! The bike crashed into the back of a fruit cart then careered off to the side. The spy on the bike cried out as he flew over the handlebars. The fruit went flying as the cart toppled over. The fruit splatted onto the cobbles and so did the spy. He'd hardly hit the ground when the police were on him.

"A few questions, if we may, sir," I heard one of them say and next thing they lifted him up and carted him off to the police station. They even took the bike. The whole exciting operation took about two minutes. I so wished I'd had my camera with me.

The man with the fruit cart was complaining loudly about his bruised and scattered fruit, so not knowing what else to do, Agnes and I ran across and helped him. We scooped up apples and blackberries, plums and pears. "For yer very kind efforts," the man said, "an orange for each of you."

"Thank you very much," we chimed, then turned to each other, oranges like trophies in our hands. "I know who would appreciate these." I said. "Elsie Noble."

We met Frank down by the river. I guessed he would be there. So was a long queue of men, all signing up to join the war effort and go to France to fight. But they were much older than Frank. He threw stones into the river while we told him the whole story: how the bike wobbled and our guest crashed into a fruit cart and how the fruit spilled everywhere. "We caught a spy," Frank said, shaking his head like he didn't believe it. "And now, hark you, here you come with blinking oranges. Wonders will never cease."

"They're for Elsie," Agnes said, "because she needs lots of vitamin C." Frank stared at her blankly. Vitamins, I found out later, hadn't been discovered yet. But suddenly Frank cheered up, like he'd remembered good news. "The police said they never did trust Gaunt. They said soon as they have despatched the suspected enemy alien to headquarters, it will be their great pleasure to bring Mr Gaunt in for questioning." Frank plonked himself down by the river and continued chucking stones in. "But I think his majesty's gone for good." He hurled another stone. "Good riddance to bad rubbish."

"How come?" I said, sitting down beside him on the grass.

"I was up early saddling his horse." Frank hurled another stone into the river. "He was all on edge, and kept telling me to get a move on. He had a wad of money stuffed in his inside pocket. I could see it alright. What a fortune. And I was thinking of all the long hours I worked myself to the bone for him, and I thought about poor Elsie, up day and night to clean for him and the paltry wages we get. Scraps instead of proper food and hardly a day off. No wonder she's ill." He threw another stone hard. "I wanted to knock him off his horse, but I kept myself under control. I heaved up his bag and strapped it to the saddle and right away felt something small and hard in the pocket of the bag." Frank smiled then lobbed another stone. "I know precious jewels when I feel them," he said slipping his hand into his jacket pocket. "If you think oranges is treasure – have a keek at this." Slowly he uncurled his fist and there it was, glinting in the morning sunshine: my mum's wedding ring! "My wages," he said and held it up to examine it. "Pure gold." Next thing he popped it in his mouth!

"Don't swallow it," I yelled.

He took it out his mouth, rubbed it on his jacket then turned it around. "Keep yer hat on mister. That's how you know it's fir real. You taste it, see. Pure Scottish gold!"

There was no easy way to say this, and I hated to disappoint him, but, "Um... Frank," I had to. "Sorry to do this to you pal, but that's actually my ring. Or, I mean, it's my mum's. Gaunt nicked it off me. And I really need it back!"

I could feel Agnes giving me her what-you-on-about look. So much had happened. I had never quite got round to telling her about my time-travelling false start. While Frank went on examining the ring and dealing with the fact that it wasn't his wages after all, Agnes tapped me on the shoulder. "But, Saul, *I've* got the ring," she said, showing me the ring on her finger.

"Yeah," I mumbled, "I know that, but..."

"But what?"

Frank was staring at us. He joined in. "But – whit?"

I had a bit of explaining to do. "Ok," I began, "it didn't work. I mean, for you, Agnes, obviously it did. Because you really, really wanted it."

"Wanted... whit?" Frank came closer. By this point I was hemmed in with Frank on one side and Agnes on the other. The river swished in front of me.

"To time travel back to 1914," Agnes told him, leaning across me. "You see, Frank, it was my idea. Saul was reluctant."

"Not totally reluctant," I chipped in. "Sure, I wanted to save the den. I mean, I am the gang leader. It just seemed – extreme!"

"Then I thought," Agnes went on, all matter of fact, "that while we were here in 1914 searching for the deeds of the house so that we could save the den, we could also learn a bit about the First World War."

"Oh," Frank said.

"I did actually try and tell you before," I said to him. "And anyway, you have to have gold."

"Gold?" said Frank.

"Yeah, and because Agnes was more focussed she went, and I got left behind." Now it was Agnes's turn to gape.

"Really?"

"Yeah! I'm trying to tell you. Then I thought you would need me, so I ran home and borrowed..." I looked meaningfully at Frank, "...my mum's wedding ring. Then sped back to the yew tree. The vapours were still going, and then the time travel worked."

Agnes gaped at me. "You sang?"

"Sure I sang. D'you think I barked or something?"

Agnes giggled then reached over and squeezed my hand. "Oh Saul, thank you so much. It would have been really hard to be here without you. I did wonder why I was in the bath for so long."

Frank scratched his nose, shook his head then went back to examining my mum's wedding ring. As if he was talking to it, he said, "You truly mean to say, with your hand on your hearts, that you... em..."

"Travelled here from a hundred years in the future." Agnes helped him out, with her hand on her heart.

"It's true, Frank," I said, hand on my heart too. "We know this ancient formula."

"To do with the elements vibrating in harmony." Agnes smiled at Frank who was looking pretty freaked out. "And the sun, and an antique song. Then of course there's the yew tree. It's associated with time."

"It's kind of... complicated," I said. "But believe it or not, it worked."

Agnes patted Frank on the knee. "And I would say to you, Frank, not to go getting involved in this war. We know what happens in this war. It's going to be terrible. It is not a sweet and lovely thing to die for your country. The poor soldiers are gassed. And shot and shelled. So many die. Really. Millions. And it is going to go on for four years. It's an awful thing. You've got your whole life ahead of you."

Frank shrugged. The reservists were queuing up over on the green. Union Jacks were flying and war fever was in the air.

"In a hundred years, Frank, life is all really different. We've got computers, and mobile phones, and... and microwaves." I was trying to change the subject but Frank didn't seem too interested in my list of technology. "And a hundred years from now, some people still have horses, and stables. And we make fires. Mostly for fun though. And we eat porridge." I wanted him to know that we weren't freaks, or aliens. We might have some newer stuff, but basically we were like him. We understood him. "Frank." I looked at him and smiled. "Thanks a lot for helping us. You've been great, really." The ring lay in his open palm. "Hey, I am so sorry about my mum's ring, because the truth is Frank, you deserve proper wages."

"And a good comfy bed," Agnes added.

"And tasty food," I said.

"And with Jean," Agnes nodded enthusiastically, "You'll get real comforts, and Elsie will too."

Frank handed me the ring. We were all silent for a moment then Frank started to laugh. There was something catching about Frank's laugh, because the next thing I started laughing. So did Agnes. Once we started we couldn't stop. We laughed so much we had tears streaming down our cheeks and we were rolling about on the grass holding our sides. Until some gentleman strode by, tapped his walking cane on the ground and roared, "Show some respect, young 'uns! Don't you know there's a war on?"

Well, the war would be on for a very long time. And here was some old guy in a bowler hat telling us to stop being happy. Frank deserved a good laugh, that was for sure. What did this old guy in a bowler hat know? Could he see the future?

When he'd strutted on, I rolled over on the grass feeling hot and sticky. It seemed forever I'd been in these clothes, working, sleeping. "I know a deep pool further up the river towards Neidpath castle," I said. "Can you swim, Frank?"

Frank grinned. "Like a dog," he boasted, and we all laughed again.

"Well – let's do it," Agnes said.

And even though there was a war on, or maybe because of it, we all jumped up and ran along the riverbank. We didn't stop running till we reached the swimming spot called the black pool.

34

"I heard about this place," Frank said, looking around the black pool and pulling off his jacket and trousers and shirt till he stood, thin and pale, in greyish saggy underwear. I saw how wiry and muscly he was. I tore off my old clothes but kept my boxers on. Frank did a double take at Homer Simpson but didn't say anything. Agnes flung her shawl onto the ground and started wriggling out of her maid's outfit. Under that long dress and apron she still had on her cut-off shorts and T-shirt. Frank made a big deal of not looking at Agnes.

"Is she going to swim?" he asked me.

"Of course," I said and poor Frank just shook his head in astonishment.

"Girls do all kinds of stuff in the future," Agnes yelled and she was the first – show-off – to run and jump into the black pool. Then she was kicking about in the water and waving wildly for me and Frank to come on in.

"You ready?" I said to Frank. He was taking deep breaths and looking down nervously. It was quite a long drop. He nodded then held out his hand. I took it and we both stepped to the edge. "One," we both yelled, "two… jump!"

And me from 2014 and Frank from 1914 jumped into the River Tweed together. Frank was right about swimming like a dog. He did the doggy paddle, with his hands clawing at the water and him not getting anywhere fast. But we had a great time, splashing and yelling and spraying each other with water. I showed Frank how to do the front crawl and he picked it up no bother. "Frank," Agnes cheered, "you swim like a fish."

"I'm a free lad," he yelled and threw up a fountain of sparkling water. He cheered like he just won a gold medal. "I'm free!"

The three of us walked back up the lane to Gaunt House; Agnes nudged me as we passed the log pile. Frank was a few steps ahead, happy, not noticing us.

"Have a look," she whispered, "they might still be there."

I tried like mad to remember which log I hid the trainers behind. One stuck out more than the rest. I slipped that one out and sure enough, there they were: my expensive, new, oh-so-comfy and very clean twenty-first-century trainers. "Yesssss!" I whispered, and hid them under my baggy jacket.

We were laughing and joking as we walked, especially Frank. "Whit's black, white and red all over?" he asked us.

I was so stunned that that joke had been on the go for one hundred years, I forgot the answer.

"A newspaper, that's whit!" he yelled.

"Knock-knock," I said, wondering if that joke had also been around for a century.

"Come in," said Frank, and me and Agnes creased ourselves laughing.

It was only when we approached the big house that the jokes dried up and we fell silent. "I hope she's rested," Frank said. His voice, that had been bawling and cheering was now all hushed. As we went through the gates and walked up the gravel driveway, the front door swung open and Mrs Buchan stepped out. She had her long brown coat on, a straw hat on her head, and she was holding a suitcase. She trotted down the steps, swinging the bag and looking well pleased with herself.

"I'll have you know," she said, as she marched towards us, "the woman you see before you will no longer stoop to dust skirting boards, run when a bell summons her, nor instruct maids in carrying chamber pots to the midden. Oh no. Mrs Buchan here has received a favourable reply. Mrs Buchan, a servant no more, is off to take up a well-paid job, supervising in the munitions factory." She strode past us, then a moment later called over her shoulder, "And do inform Mr Gaunt that he can find himself another housekeeper: one fool enough to work for pennies!" And with that she strode through the gates that Frank had left open, and marched off into the big wide world.

"We will enter through the front doors, for once in our lives," Frank said, and that's what we did. Gaunt House felt even stranger than usual. It was eerily quiet.

"Our American guest has gone," Agnes whispered as we crossed the large empty entrance hall and gazed up the stairway.

"He wasn't American," I reminded her, "and he wasn't a proper guest either."

We passed the famous coat stand. Gaunt had left his precious cape behind. "The owner's gone too," Agnes whispered and before I could say anything she said, "who wasn't even the proper owner."

Frank called out, "Elsie! Elsie!"

We practically fell into the kitchen, panting and puffing, and there was Elsie up at the table wrapped in a tartan shawl, chopping onions. "Lord above!" she cried out, dropping her knife. "What took you? They'll be crying out for hen broth I'm sure and you've all been gallivanting, leaving poor Elsie to all the chores. What's Gaunt going to say, eh? When there is no broth made?" She sunk down onto a wooden chair with a great sigh, as if the effort of speaking was all too much.

"We brought you oranges," Agnes said, placing hers on the table. I set mine next to it.

"Lord above, it's Christmas!" Elsie murmured, and burst into tears.

"It is like Christmas," Agnes said, putting an arm around her shoulder. "Dear Elsie, you must pack your bags because as soon as you and Frank have your things ready, we can go. Jean is waiting for you. She'll give you a good home and make you better. Don't cry, Elsie."

While Frank comforted his sister and set about packing up their few belongings, Agnes and I slipped outside. It was time to have a good look at the yew tree.

35

We circled the yew tree, trying to see where the grass might have been dug, or maybe stones loosened, or some kind of marking to show where the deeds might be hidden. There was a small patch where the grass was a slightly lighter green. This would turn mossy a hundred years from now.

Agnes sunk to her knees and patted the hard ground. Gnarled roots from the tree bumped up round the trunk.

"The grass is different here," I said, sinking to my knees and patting the spot. 'The roots of the yew hold fast' the newspaper article had said. I stroked the knotted roots, pretty certain that the deeds of this land were hidden just below. Agnes patted them too.

We looked at each other.

"Uh huh," said Agnes. "I think we've found everything we needed to find in 1914."

Then she winked at me, whipped the key from her pocket and scaled the tree like an acrobat. Moments later she was back, panting and flushed-looking. "So my great-great-great grandfather hid the deeds under the tree. I've hidden the key in the branches." We left the tree and ran together back up to the house. "You never know," she said, laughing, "but it just might come in handy!"

Frank and Elsie didn't have much to pack. We said we'd walk them down to the gates.

"I won't miss this big gloomy house one bit," Elsie said as we stepped through the front door. "I won't even look back."

"Quite right," Frank said. Elsie was wearing a long brown dress – her Sunday best, she told us and Frank was in a black jacket. Elsie hadn't coughed once. Maybe the two days in bed had done her some good.

"I don't care if the house crumbles to the ground," Frank said and just to help it along he slammed the huge wooden door. I heard something inside fall – the coat stand! Then I imagined how wallpaper would peel. Damp would eat into everything. Oak beams would crack and, stone by stone, this mansion house would fall to the ground.

"Right then," Frank said, beaming at us, and he marched off down the drive. "I said my farewells," he called over his shoulder, "to the gardener and Trickster. The gardener says how he's going to stay on, living in his hut, tending the garden, so long as no one throws him out. He'll take care of Trickster too."

"I don't think anyone will throw him out. No one can," Agnes said.

"I heard from the farmer who brings the milk that the police are looking for Gaunt. I don't think he'll be back, and if he's stupid enough to come creeping around, they'll be ready for him. He's been harbouring a German spy. I told you, didn't I? I said he'd get his comeuppance. Come on, Saul and Agnes, keep up!"

We had stopped to look back. All those clean windows and no one watching us go. "Shame, isn't it?" Agnes said, "That Yew Tree House is going to crumble and fall."

"But lucky for us," I said, "the hut will stay, and so will the yew tree."

Frank and Elsie were waiting at the gates. "Reckon they'll smelt this lot down into rifles," Frank said, tapping one of the iron bars.

"I reckon you're right, Frank," I said, "because I can tell you, the gates didn't make it into the future."

Elsie gazed up at me, wide-eyed. "Gosh, Frank told me. All I can say is… it's a miracle."

"You're right," Agnes said, stepping across to an oak tree by the wall. "Time travel is a miracle." She climbed up that tree and was down a minute later with her trusty rucksack. "And soon," she announced, "the time travellers are going home." She hoisted the rucksack onto her back.

Everything was beginning to feel like a dream. It was as if things were already fading, like when you see people leave on a boat, and they get smaller and smaller. That was how it felt. Frank was talking about going past the railway station on their way to Jean's, so they could see all the soldiers in brown uniforms and women waving hankies, and they could join in the cheering. He was marching back and forth with their old suitcase: left-right, left-right. Stopping to salute and marching again.

Agnes put an arm around Elsie's shoulder. "You can take it easy, Elsie. Jean will care for you." Then Agnes called out to Frank, "You don't have to march, Frank. Come and say goodbye."

He stopped and swung round. "You dinnae understand, Agnes. If it's true whit you say, and you really do come from the future, there are some things you just dinnae understand. I do have to march." He practised again, swinging his arms, holding his head up high. As I watched him, left-right, left-right, marching towards us, I knew he was right. There were things about really living in 1914 that we just didn't understand.

Agnes gave Elsie a hug. Frank and me glanced across at each other and it struck me how this was goodbye, and how I would miss him. He nodded, like he was thinking the same. "Yea've been a great friend, Saul," he said. "Brave and good fun. We worked well together, you and me. I want tae thank yea for whit yea've done for us."

"You too, Frank," I said, and we shook hands, then laughed. Then he picked up his bag, waved to me, took Elsie's arm and they walked on across the field. Somehow, because of all the work, I'd always thought of Elsie and Frank as small grown-ups, but now, walking away to their new life, they looked like us. Agnes and me watched them go.

"Good luck," I shouted.

"Good luck to you too," Frank and Elsie turned round and waved to us. Me and Agnes waved back, until finally they stopped waving and walked on. Then they were gone, into a Peebles just at the beginning of the First World War.

"Well, Agnes," I turned to look at her, "are you ready?"

She wiped a tear from her cheek and smiled. "I'm ready, gang leader." As we walked along the road she patted her rucksack and winked at me, "And we've got everything time travellers need, right in here."

As a parting gesture, like an actor hanging up his costume when the play's over, I left my patched-up 1914 suit at the back door of Yew Tree House, and hung the cap on the doorknob. I put my trainers on over my filthy feet. Agnes had stuffed her brown dress into the rucksack and was now busy at the tree setting up the elements. She had tucked the wilted white rose Jean had given her behind her hair. "For luck," she said, winking, though I was pretty sure we couldn't bring things into the future.

Because I was a bit of an expert now, I made the fire, and Agnes set her wee pan of water on the flames for the steam. I looked about for the gardener but couldn't see him. Looking dirty but more like our usual selves, we pressed our hands one over the other against the bark of the yew tree. "Double gold, double power," I said, and both rings glinted in the sun. The glass globe spun. Steam turned the rainbows into swirling, coloured mist. I looked down, hoping like mad that we really were standing on the buried deeds, and that no one would find them, not for a hundred years.

"So, who's going to sing the antique song then," Agnes whispered.

"You start", I said, "and I'll join in."

She did and the ring felt hot on my little finger and pretty soon I started to feel dizzy. In the distance I thought I could hear the horse whinny. I imagined it all alone in the stable, and the gardener all alone in the big garden. The house was empty. But the den wasn't. My head started to spin. The wind moaned. The gardener was going to have the horse. Tricksie, or Trickstar, or whatever it was called. Maybe the army would take the horse? Maybe... The ground under my feet seemed to sway and I tried to sing but my voice sounded like it was far away. The needles of the yew swished in the strong wind. The song turned into a ringing in my ears. Everything went black and I felt like I was falling.

36

And I kept on falling.

Like I was jumping off the river bank into the black pool but the jump was going on for ever and there was ash puffing up into the air and flames flickering and a rod coming loose on a bike brake and fruit spilling all over the street and a scratchy blanket and porridge and potatoes and Frank saluting and Elsie frowning and a horse neighing in the stable and Agnes singing on the street then a scuffle and swimming in the river and Agnes splashing and shouting, "Don't go to war, Frank!", and him yelling he was free...

"What happened to your T-shirt?"

"Jeez Louise, did you ever see such a manky face?"

"I think they fainted. Maybe we should chuck a bucket of water over them."

"Your theory is rubbish, Will. Like, they've been gone 23 minutes. A minute you said. Saul! Saul, can you hear me?"

I could, but I couldn't move. I tried to open my eyes but it felt like they were glued. I wanted to speak but I couldn't. Part of me was still falling... and Jean was waving, and she had a flower in her hair, and the soldiers were smiling, and the women were waving hankies, they were saying they'd be home for Christmas… but they'd be gassed, and lame, and blind…

"Agnes! What happened to your flip-flops?"

She groaned. Then I heard her mumble, "I think… I lost them in the field." Then I managed to open my eyes and the first thing I saw was Robbie's face but it was going round and round, like it was in a washing machine and I felt Agnes shake me. "You ok?"

I hoisted myself up onto my elbows and looked at her. Slowly the world stopped spinning. She was sitting beside me on the grass under the tree, looking dazed. The white rose had gone. "If I have a good scout around," she was muttering, "then maybe the flip-flops will be under the grass, somewhere…"

And I remembered what else was buried under the grass. "You know that old rusty garden spade?" I mumbled to Robbie and Will. My voice had caught up with me. I was all in one piece.

"Saul! We were seriously worried. Like, more than twenty minutes you've been gone. I was going to get the police, or your mum," Robbie was saying. "Will ate all the crisps by the way. We waited in the den, but you didn't turn up. So we ran down to the tree. The glass globe was still swinging and the fire was still alight. It freaked me out. I mean, where were you?"

"I'll tell you later," I said, "but right now, do you think you could go and get that spade?" I would have run to the den and got it myself, except my knees were shaking and my feet had pins and needles.

"Oh yeah," Agnes yelled, "the deeds! And the key!"

"The what?" Now it was Will and Robbie yelling their heads off. "Did you find them? Can you save the den?"

Shakily I got to my feet. I had to lean against the yew tree to steady myself. Robbie was right: the glass globe was still swinging and the bonfire was still glowing. I helped Agnes up. "Maybe we did," I muttered. Maybe we didn't, I thought. "Get the spade and we'll find out."

"You look like you just ran a marathon or something," Will said. "Saul, are you ok? I mean, do you want a coke, or sweets, or a macaroni pie or something?"

"Look, Will, if you could just get that spade..."

"I mean, I'm pretty sure this kind of time travel is dangerous," Robbie said. "Like, amazingly risky. I know you've got this formula and all that, but... me and Will were seriously worried. It felt like hours."

"I appreciate you were worried," I said. "But are you gonna get that spade? Because then we'll dig for treasure."

"Sure," they both said and raced each other up the garden to the den.

"I hope they're here," I said, gazing at the mossy patch under the tree.

Agnes dropped to her knees and started patting the ground. "Looks pretty much like it did a hundred years ago," she said. "Undisturbed. So if John Hogg buried them here, I reckon they're still here."

When Will and Robbie came running back up the garden, Robbie with the old spade in his hands, and Will with what looked like a huge bag of popcorn, I asked Agnes what her dad would do with the land. "Oh, nothing," she said, breezily, "he likes living in the caravan. Says the simple life is a happy life. And he says he likes wild places, like this." She looked around at the ruined house and the overgrown garden. It felt weird to see it back to its old ruined mess. "Don't worry, Saul," she said, smiling up at me. "He'll leave it just the way it is."

Agnes pointed to the mossy patch under the yew tree. Robbie and Will stood by. As gang leader, I was the one to do the digging. I wedged the heel of my foot – safe in my trainers – against the edge of the spade. I had this sudden fear that there was going to be nothing there. I glanced at Agnes. By the way she chewed her lip and pulled at her hair I guessed she had the same fear. "Even if it turns out there's nothing there," she said, "it was still worth it."

She was right about that. I thought about Frank and Elsie and the German spy and I pushed the spade down through the mossy earth. Deeds or no deeds, the time travel had been worth it. The ground was soft and it cut in easily, though I didn't hear it hit against any treasure chest. "It's probably really deep," Will said, upbeat. "I mean, if it's been there for over a hundred years, it would have sunk." I didn't know if Will's theory was right but I dug deeper. I felt strong – probably after carting all that coal.

"Keep going, Saul," Agnes said. She wasn't twisting her hair round her finger now. She was peering down into the hole I was making. I pushed the spade deeper, and deeper, and then it hit something.

I yelled.

"That's it!" Agnes cried.

"Could be a stone," I panted.

"It doesn't look like a stone." Agnes flashed her torch down the hole. I pulled back the spade and peered in. Agnes fell to her knees, training her torch on some light-coloured thing. "I think... it looks like... a tin," she called up, her voice shaking. She peered closer. "A biscuit tin! Saul – do you want to bring it up?"

I leant on the spade, my heart racing. "You bring it up, if you want," I said.

She looked up at me, her eyes shining. "Yes, I do want to." Then she lay right down on the ground and stretched her arms down the hole. Robbie and Will were jumping up and down like frogs and I was gripping the spade so tight my knuckles went white. I watched Agnes bring up a rusty, cream-coloured tin box covered in earth. I watched her place the box carefully on the grass and brush some of the soil off it. I watched her dig her nails under the lid and try to pull it open. Her face was turning red with the effort. "It won't... budge," she cried.

"It's got a keyhole!" I cried out. "There, under the handle. Where's the key from the secret passage?"

Agnes leapt up and, looking less dazed and more determined, scrambled up into the yew, disappearing up into its thick dark branches. Above us, the branches shook. A minute later she was back down again with John Hogg's key, her eyes shining.

"It's rusted, Saul, but it was still there," she said.

Rubbing it down, she worked it into the keyhole, and turned it. It clicked.

Then Will knelt down to help. So did Robbie. I let the spade fall and sunk to my knees beside them. "One," we all yelled, feeling the lid give slightly, "two…" It moved a tiny bit more. "Three!"

37

The box lid sprang open and there they were – old documents wrapped in red ribbons and stating, so Agnes read in a trembling voice:

The mansion house known as Yew Tree House by Eshiels Bank, Peebles, in the county of Peebleshire, in the country of Scotland, and the land of one acre surrounding it, is the sole property of Mr John Hogg and in the event of his death the said property will pass to the next male heir – by Scots Law.

Signed by witnesses

Dr Gray

and

Messrs Strachan

Peebles, Michaelmas, 1874

"We've done it," Agnes murmured, gazing round at our very own wild and fabulous garden. "We've actually done it." The deeds shook in her hand. "My dad is the next male heir. We've saved the den!"

Agnes was right about her dad. He said it gave him unspeakable delight to send these money-grabbing property developers packing. He said it was enough that his only daughter had lost her mother, she didn't need to lose her childhood too. And children, he said, need places to play. Wild and wonderful places! Me, Will and Robbie put our pocket money together and bought Agnes's dad a huge box of chocolates and he said we were the best pals Agnes could wish for.

The story got out that we had found the buried title deeds and there was even a bit about it in the local paper.

CHILDREN AT PLAY DISCOVER LOST DEEDS TO LAND

Thankfully we didn't have swarms of photographers nosing around the den. The bulldozers turned round and trundled off. The luxury homes developers looked for some other piece of land to build on, and things went back to normal. We climbed trees, played hide and seek, swung on the rope swing, made fires and munched on toasted marshmallows.

During one game of cards we were chatting about

doing a bit of artwork in the den. "Funny, isn't it?" Robbie said, gazing about, "that this den is in way better nick than the ruined house."

"I've been wondering that too," Agnes said, flicking down an ace of spades and trumping us. "So – I did a bit of research."

I felt my heart sink. "And?" She had told me she was going to the museum. She had asked me if I wanted to go with her. She had told me she was going to read all the names on the war memorial. But I had said I didn't feel like going. "Reluctant, Saul?" she had said, winking at me. But it wasn't that. I just wanted to keep them all young. Sometimes when I woke in the middle of the night they were there, Frank and Elsie. Frank would be laughing, maybe nicking a piece of cake, and Elsie would be playing snap, and I didn't want to change that.

Agnes scooped up the cards and told us what she had found out. "Jack Lamb, a retired gardener and hermit, lived in this hut alone until 1964. He was eighty-five years old when the authorities found him and decided to move him into a home where he died three days later." We all looked about our den as if the ghost of Jack Lamb might suddenly appear. I noticed things about our den I hadn't seen before; like places where wood had been added, and holes patched up. "It said in the obituary I read," Agnes went on, "that Mr Lamb took good care of the few things he had. He lived by trapping rabbits, catching pheasants and growing fruit and vegetables."

"Thanks very much, Mr Jack," Robbie said, nodding appreciatively to our surroundings.

"And – I found out other stuff," Agnes said, shuffling the cards.

I shot a glance at my watch. "But you know what," I blurted out. "I was supposed to be home five minutes ago to pack for France."

"France!" Will and Robbie cheered.

"*Demain*," said Agnes, jumping to her feet and grinning, "*nous allons à Paris!*"

"We'll climb the Eiffel Tower," Will yelled as we all wriggled through the hole in the wall and set off over the field.

"And go on all the rides at Disneyland," Robbie cheered.

"And don't forget the art galleries," Agnes chirped.

In all our cheering and laughing, not one of us mentioned the trip to the war graves in northern France. The teacher, Mrs Johnston, had said it was fitting at this time to spend half a day there and no one dared complain. She said how we would visit the Gardens of Remembrance and cast our minds back one hundred years. Agnes and I had shot each other a look across the classroom. We had more memories than Mrs Johnston could ever imagine.

38

We did the Eiffel Tower which was really high and from the top you had this terrific view of the whole of Paris, and we went on a boat down the river Seine. I didn't need to get worried about frog's legs because in France we ate pretty much the same food as in Scotland, just with more bread and cheese. Agnes made us all practise our French until we were fluent in, "*Bonjour – nous sommes Eccossais.*" Very loudly. And we did go to the Louvre art gallery, even though we had to queue for a whole hour to get in. When we eventually got in Agnes led us straight to the Mona Lisa, and Robbie said it was tiny and she said small can be powerful and beautiful, and the woman in the painting smiled at us, like she knew secrets about us all. Robbie and Will went off to spend five euros on a hot chocolate and, with the Mona Lisa's eyes still following me, Agnes led me off to see another famous painting – of sunflowers in a vase.

"I've been waiting for the right time to tell you," she whispered while crowds peered over our heads to get a glimpse of the famous sunflowers.

"Tell me what?" I whispered though I had a pretty good idea. She fumbled about in her little bag and drew out a sheet of paper. "I got this from the war records in the museum in Peebles," she whispered. "You ready?"

I nodded, but kept on staring at the bright golden painted sunflowers while she read out very quietly:

```
Private  Frank  Noble  was  killed  in
action  at  the  battle  of  the  Somme  in
Northern  France,  1st  July  1916.  Said  to
be  nineteen,  it  was  later  discovered
Private  Noble  was  in  fact  just  sixteen
years  of  age.  As  well  as  making  the
great  sacrifice  while  serving  his
country,  Noble  will  be  remembered  for
the  part  he  played  in  uncovering  the
German  spy,  Herr  Loden.  Noble  was
survived  by  his  twin  sister,  Elspeth
Noble  of  Walkershaugh,  Peebles.
```

Agnes folded up the sheet of paper and put it back in her bag. The sunflowers looked like they wanted to burst out of the vase. They were like trumpets playing a victory song.

"They were twins," Agnes whispered. "Can you believe it, Saul? Frank and Elsie were twins! Elsie survived. I read how she lived with Jean Burns until 1930 when she flitted to Edinburgh. I read how Elspeth Noble fought for women's rights to education and decent pay. Good old Elsie. I always knew she was a fighter. Both of them were. And they were only fourteen, back then. When we knew them."

Back then seemed like a very long time ago. Like

another lifetime. We both stared up at the painting and didn't say anything for a while.

Then Agnes nudged me, held up a ten euro note and whispered, "Hot chocolate?"

"We'll toast them," I said, as we walked through the crowded gallery in search of a café. "We'll drink to the memory of Frank and Elsie."

"And Jean," Agnes said.

"And all the soldiers," I whispered. And as we hurried through the gallery I remembered how Frank had marched right-left, right-left, and how he was itching to join those soldiers, get on a train, wear a uniform and serve his country.

"You know what?" I said to Agnes as we sat down at a café table, "I think I'll have a cup of tea instead. Coz you know," I winked at her, "there's nothing like a guid cup o' tea fir pitting the world tae rights." And when our tea arrived, me and Agnes rose to our feet. "Wet yer whistle on a guid cup o tea, Agnes," I said, and clinking our teacups together we toasted them: "To Frank! A brave soldier of the First World War! And to Elsie, who also fought for freedom!"

39

On the last day of the school trip we went to the Gardens of Remembrance. Our coach stopped at a place called Thiepval at the Somme in Northern France. We all gathered round a massive monument, which was to the memory of the missing, lost in the battle of the Somme. There was a soldier playing a bugle. The teacher said he was playing a tune called 'The Last Post'. There were 74,000 names written on that monument, and one of them was Frank Noble's. Behind it were rows and rows of small white marble crosses. This garden was one of the cemeteries of the war dead, the teacher told us, in a very hushed voice. She said that many were buried where they fell and many were never found. And this is just one cemetery, she told us, with 7,000 graves. There were many more.

Mrs Johnston said we should walk around a bit and remember. And though there were loads of people milling around it was eerily quiet. No one was talking. Some of the graves marked by white crosses had names on them. Most didn't. But they all said:

A soldier of the Great War
Known unto God

Me and Agnes wandered off to the edge of a field and sat for a while – remembering Frank. We walked back to the coach in silence. The teacher was ushering pupils back into the bus and still everybody was quiet. When we were all in our seats the teacher stood up in the front of the bus. "Before we leave," she said, "and head for Calais and Scotland, I would like to recite a short poem. It was written by Lawrence Binyon in August 1914, when this terrible war had only just begun." Agnes and I glanced at each other.

"They shall not grow old as we that are left grow old:
Age shall not weary them, nor the years condemn.
At the going down of the sun and in the morning,
We will remember them."

The coach took us on to the ferry at Calais. It was only when the boat left France and the bobbing waves were under us that we started chatting. Leaning over the rails we waved to France. Then we went in to get chips smothered in mayonnaise and Robbie got out the red scarf he had bought for his mum. I showed everyone the black French beret I got for my dad and Agnes passed round the silvery Eiffel Tower statue she had bought for her gran. She said she also bought one to put up in the den and we all cheered, and suddenly I couldn't wait to get home and see my mum and dad, the twins – and the den! It was our den. It was saved, and we planned to hang out in it all summer long.

Then we all ran out onto the deck and Agnes shouted that she could see the white cliffs of Dover in the distance.

"A few more hours and we'll be in Scotland," I yelled.

This reluctant time traveller was going home.

AFTERWORD

Carl Hans Lody was one of the most famous spies of the First World War. Posing as Mr Charles A. Inglis from New York, with a false American passport, he was in fact a German secret agent. He made his way to Scotland at the outbreak of the First World War, to spy on the naval bases there. He spent one night in The County Hotel in Peebles, before setting off by bicycle the next morning for the naval base at Leith, near Edinburgh, in the Firth of Forth. His coding letters, sent to Sweden, were eventually intercepted by code breakers, but not before many had died because of his spying. His codes were found to be fairly simple to break. They were similar to the description in this book. On arrest, a German coin was found on Lody's person, along with a German dry-cleaning stub. He was arrested and executed by firing squad at dawn at the Tower of London on November 6th, 1914.

ACKNOWLEDGEMENTS

The Reluctant Time Traveller is a work of fiction, though some of the story is informed by fact. For these facts of early twentieth-century history and the First World War, my thanks go to Peebles Museum for information about Peebles, and to a number of authors who have written about the First World War, most notably Theresa Breslin in *Remembrance* and Olivia Dent in *A Volunteer Nurse on the Western Front*. Thanks also to Nicola Wright, storyteller and tour guide, for information about the Gardens of Remembrance at Thiepval in northern France. For images of service and the life of servants, thanks to my own grandmother, who was 'in service,'; and to *Downton Abbey*, plus many books on the subject. For talking with me about Peebles, education and history, thanks to the teachers of Kingsland Primary School. For knowledge on how to tamper with a 1914 bike, thanks to my dad, Ramsay Mackay. For his poem 'Dulce et Decorum Est', thanks to Wilfred Owen. For his poem 'They shall not grow old', thanks to Lawrence Binyon.

And to the enduring memory of those who did not grow old in the First World War.

Also by Janis Mackay

THE MAGNUS FIN TRILOGY

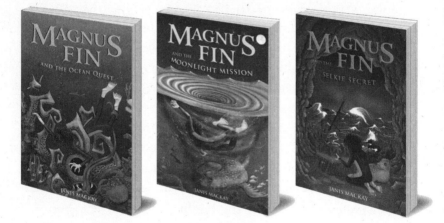

Three exciting underwater adventures starring Magnus Fin, the eleven-year-old half-selkie (part-human, part-seal) hero.

 Also available as eBooks

discoverkelpies.co.uk